MONSTERS

PAUL MELNICZEK

King's Way Press
2019

FIRST EDITION

MONSTERS © 2019 by Paul Melniczek
Cover Art © 2019 by Glenn Chadbourne

Cover and interior design by
Zombie Book Design

King's Way Press
www.kwp-books.com

FOREWARD

Monsters.

There have always existed tales throughout mankind's history which have detailed fantastic creatures, ones which defy our understanding. Mountain, forest, lake, and sea alike, there is no boundary or frontier which has not been touched by their presence in some way.

They are referenced everywhere, seen everywhere. Both ancient and modern civilizations describe their existence. In tribal tales, urban folklore, religious texts, and rustic superstition. The roots run deep, and are expansive enough to cover the entire world. Great beasts and serpents, terrible and wondrous to behold. And dangerous to those unfortunate enough to encounter them.

Where did these stories come from? Who created them? Why? The explanations are as varied as the tales themselves. In truth, we don't really know. Metaphorical or metaphysical? Decide for yourself.

One can certainly deny the reality of these creatures, but not the *fact* that such stories do indeed exist, and will continue to do so. There is even evidence that some tales are based on actual species, ones which were eventually discovered and documented scientifically. For the vast majority, though, the proof is elusive. It's easy, even practical, to wave off these stories in our modern world, beneath the light of day.

But what about at night? While we're alone? Or in faraway lands and isolated regions, sections of which have yet to be traveled and explored? Perceptions can quickly change if circumstances permit, and deeply buried fears arise. With the shrinking of our world due to technology, there has evolved a natural progression of enlightenment, further banishing tales of things which lurk in the shadows. Mankind has set foot upon every part of our world, and has reached for the stars in the eternal quest for knowledge.

Then why do these stories persist?

Are they all to be passed off as nonsense, and imagination? Skeptics would have us think so.

But science can't explain away everything. How much of the vast universe have we traveled? In reality, none of it.

There are infinite worlds to explore in the endless reaches of space and time, so much that the collective dreaming of our race will never come close to imagining even the smallest piece of its entirety. It's a wonderful and romantic pursuit, though. And this thirst for answers makes us what we are.

Human.

With all our human traits and emotions, our hopes and fears.

Some say our fascination of monsters is an inherent need to latch onto something unknown as we release more answers to the mysteries of the universe. Others think it's a primordial reaction from darker times, when we lacked our modern illumination to keep the demons of twilight at bay.

Either way, they remain with us. They are our unlikely companions across the years; the chaos to our order, the ugliness to our beauty, the nightmare to our dreams. And whether you believe in them or not, they will never be dispelled.

At times, strange things happen to us and we ultimately discover that they originate from natural sources.

But sometimes not...

We can't always find explanations for all of our experiences and encounters with unknown creatures.

And whether they materialize physically from beneath the shroud of darkness, or psychically from within the closeted recesses of our mind, they linger alongside of us. Try as we like, we can never entirely escape from their terrible clutch or mesmerizing call.

They remain, waiting for the time and place when we're most vulnerable, to emerge once more.

Monsters.

And so, inside the pages of this book, I'll share with you my own personal vision of these unknown creatures. I'll lead you on a journey into lands both strange and hostile, others strikingly familiar, and we'll travel together on a quest for answers.

But be careful what you wish for...

WHITE

Parker paused for a moment, tightening the rope about his waist and taking advantage of the brief halt. His two guides chattered in their native dialect, pointing to the ridge directly above them. He glanced over his shoulder, retracing the path which had brought them here to such a high altitude. Blankets of perpetual snow covered the landscape, giving it the appearance of a forlorn, alien planet, isolated and forbidding. Only a few hours had passed since they'd left the tiny mountain village, but it could have been on the other side of the world for all that mattered. Mist obscured most of the vista in every direction except for the deep ravine to their left which ended in white oblivion. Parker felt the remoteness of their location as a subtle, almost tangible presence of its own, something vast and ancient, waiting patiently to swallow the unwary.

Here he was an outsider, trespassing in a pristine sanctuary that would always exist beyond man's control, an untamable region that might let a select few travelers enter of their own free will, but their fate was uncertain, held hostage by the land's unrestful tendency towards chaos. Parker knew all these things for fact and respected them. Despite this awareness of his predicament, it did nothing to alleviate the invisible fingers of fear which had nudged him since their ascent had begun, weighing heavily on his heart and refusing to let go.

Rijak signaled for the group to continue, and Parker focused on the trek at hand, mentally shrugging off his apprehension. He'd come too far to let anything shake his focus, and his determination was strong. The company of men was small; himself and Carlton Rogers—his assistant and best friend—along with the guides, the other a younger man named Liyar, who spoke no English at all. The two made a stalwart pair, eyes constantly scanning the horizon for their chosen path as well as any potential dangers, which were many. It hadn't been easy to secure these two. In fact, none other from the village would have anything to do with their expedition.

The local inhabitants were a tough breed, resourceful but friendly enough, if a bit reserved at first. And superstitious?

To the very bone...

Except for their two hired men, the rest of the villagers never traveled this high. They seemed to be on the very brink of the sky itself.

They resumed the hike, their insulated boots crunching into the packed snow and ice, and Parker fought against the illusion that they were actually walking in place and going nowhere. He'd certainly faced extreme conditions before and other climbs, but none as intimidating as his present circumstances. The Himalayans were truly one of the world's most demanding frontiers, treacherous and mysterious. Of course, the severe location was the very reason that he now found himself here, looking for answers to puzzling questions, ones which kept him awake at night with eyes open wide and mind racing. Parker was on a fact-finding mission, and if successful, his place would be assured among the world's premier scientific journalists.

But the path had not been easy, the preparations lengthy and at great cost. This region was an unforgiving one, where the living fell victim to the clutches of a cold and barren landscape which had no equal. In spite of the harshness, a few rugged species had managed to survive...*Survive.* Here of all places, finding ways to adapt, etch out a fragile existence.

There were langur monkeys, red bear, snow leopards. Rare finds for anyone traversing the area, especially at such high altitudes. Yet they existed. These creatures, and *just* maybe something else even more elusive and strange. Unknown to man, except in legends spoken by the natives who dared make this place their home amidst the very ceiling of the world itself. In hushed tones they would whisper amongst themselves as they huddled around campfires on frigid nights when the wind howled and ice fell in stinging clumps. They made sure to keep their voices down lest the dreadful mountain spirits would catch their conversation and take heed.

They had a name for it.

Among the indigenous population, the Tibetans, it was called the Kanchenjunga Demon. And to others, like Parker or his open-minded colleagues, it was known by another name.

The Yeti.

By the time they reached the encampment two hours had passed, the sky darkening considerably as a premature nightfall descended. The structure fell far short of being a real base or camp, as it consisted of a wooden foundation with stout uprights hammered into the frozen ground, allowing for them to attach their tent. In this fashion it saved much time and added great convenience, despite its primitiveness. Parker and Carlton were not going to argue though…There had been few moments of any comfort on their journey so far. The long boat ride overseas had been an adventure in itself, with many uneasy nights. Both of them had suffered bouts of illness due to poor drinking water within the past week, and an unpleasant scrape with local government officials was still within recent memory. Parker's journal was filled with notes long and short as he accounted for every single mile of their trek, pouring all his emotion into the sights and wonders of Central Asia and its peculiar inhabitants. The lowland jungles which fed on the liquid vitality which gushed forth from the Himalayan Plateau. The pristine mountain lakes filled with water which sparkled like the jewels in Solomon's Crown when struck by rays from the afternoon sun, the sky a brilliant blue so glorious that it had no name in any language. Vast glaciers which could consume the very earth itself if given the time of the ages. Buddhist temples perched precariously above yawning crevices like petrified birds of prey.

What they had experienced up to this point would make for an article both enlightening and captivating. It had already been the excursion of a lifetime which few would ever be witness to.

But it was not enough…Parker needed more. Something which would shake the foundations of science to its very roots and unbalance the skeptics, quench their mockery. Many of his colleagues had scoffed at his undertaking. Some kept their opinions close by taking a neutral position, but a select few had given him their forthright support, admiring his determination. And although it would be extremely satisfying to look his detractors in the eye and prove them wrong, he cared more about those who had put their unwavering faith in him. People like Jaspin Myer, Rogers Greth, and Sir William Riceborough. Most of all, he wanted to see the look of confirmation on *their* faces, the ones who believed in Parker and his quest.

The guides quickly unpacked and went about getting the tent set up while Parker spoke with Carlton. "That was a tough climb, my friend."

Carlton nodded, leaning forward and rubbing his legs. "Stiff as a board. How much further do you intend on going tomorrow? Do you think we may be high enough yet?"

"Well, from what they've told me, we've actually reached the very edge of their sacred land. We've now traveled to a point where even the locals have never been." Parker spread his arms for emphasis. "Isn't that amazing? And these two alone from the village will climb to here, but *not* beyond that ridge. So there must be a reason behind this." He nodded emphatically, his blue eyes intense. "I think we've reached our destination. After all these past weeks, all our troubles to get this far. We've arrived. And what a fantastic world we've stumbled into..."

It *was* an incredible scene around them. Nothing but milky whiteness in every direction, with brief glimpses of the peak jutting upwards through the mist, leading towards the unattainable summit beyond. Other travelers, serious climbers, might have tried to go higher. A handful had in previous years returned to tell the tale of their fateful venture. They were the fortunate ones. Their companions lay buried beneath ice and stone, as much a part of the mountain as anything else here, both in body and spirit, resting the deep sleep until the end of time itself, or when the world changed and the mighty Himalayans crumbled into the sea. The landscape was incredibly daunting, and the spell of the mountain had fallen upon both men—silent, vast, and implacable. The excitement of their predicament churned like a river through Parker's veins, but he also trembled inside from an even greater sensation—one of isolation, the feeling that they had entered into a forbidden sanctuary and were temporarily permitted only because they were too insignificant to be of any concern.

He drew in his breath, the sharp air biting his lungs through his protective mask. The unpleasant sentiment faded, but not entirely. His determination remained steadfast, and he was cautious, as of a man who knowingly lingered at the edge of a cave which housed a sleeping bear, making care not to bring attention to himself and arouse the slumbering beast.

They ate a light meal and drank from their pouches, sharing wine with their two guides. Few words were spoken as they huddled around the small fire, basking in its warmth. Several times Parker referred to the area beyond the ridge, but this only made the men fidget nervously.

Liyar even made some odd gestures at one point, and Parker recognized them as symbols to ward off evil. Not necessarily superstitious himself, it did succeed to increase his own apprehension, although the logical part of him argued that the dangers here were from environmental concerns, and none other. The conversation eventually dwindled as they all succumbed to fatigue one by one, Parker's last waking memory one of staring into the cinders from the fire, and imagining he saw a pair of crimson eyes staring right back at him.

《《—》》

The hour was late when Parker was roused from sleep, and he found himself gazing into the dwindling embers, his skin rolling with goose-flesh at what he'd been dreaming. But when he saw the frightened eyes of the two guides he knew the source came from *elsewhere*, and not his own slumbering fantasies, and this fact shook him to the very bone.

His mouth opened in question. "What is it…"

Then he stopped, listening to something which *should* not be in that most isolated of places, yet it existed—a sound from outside the tent, far off in the distance, but discernible against the rushing wind.

It was enough to make Parker's blood run cold. A low wailing, as of a lost soul in anguish, yet clearly not human, more like a wild beast of some kind. The look on the guides' faces was one of pure terror in its most primeval of roots. They whispered strange words, Liyar quivering in fear.

Carlton still lay asleep, and Parker was too mesmerized to awaken him as he sat there, straining to hear more of the fantastic sound. Long moments passed as they waited there in silence, the weight of the mountain and the *unknown* pressing in against their fragile camp as a palpable, living presence. Parker felt his pulse racing, his heart pounding in his chest, the memory of the incredible sound echoing in his mind. What *was* it? What was out there? Could it be the legendary creature he had come so far to find?

He made a move towards the flap of the tent, but Rijak grabbed his arm, holding him. "*Must* stay inside…"

The intensity on the guide's face needed no further verbal confirmation to back it up. It was clear that Parker would not be permitted to go past the confines of their small camp. And what would he see regardless? It was night, visibility would be non-existent, and whatever had made the sound would be a good distance away. The only rational thing to do was wait until morning so he could investigate in the light, hope to come across signs of what had been out there, maybe locate tracks of some type. It made sense, and in reality, any other course of action would have been foolhardy, if not downright dangerous. He knew it, and now backed down. But a part of him also wondered if he even possessed the courage to pass through the small slit in the canvas and enter into the outer darkness knowing what *might* be out there...

Sleep eluded the three men for the remainder of the night. Parker was motionless for a long period of time, striving in vain to hear more, but the mountain was now silent, having let the intruders catch a fleeting glimpse of something which lay hidden, preferring the high places of the world well beyond the reach of men. Whatever had made the noise was gone, either oblivious to their presence, or tolerant. Or perhaps waiting...

Parker watched as Rijak kept the fire going, at times throwing small pieces of wood onto it to prolong its life. The guide was quiet, offering nothing. No explanation or further warning. And sometime earlier, Parker had seen (or perhaps sensed) a change in the man. A relaxation of tenseness, as if they'd entered a period of danger which had now passed. Parker wanted to press him with questions, grab the man by the shoulders and demand answers, but realized that he would get nothing from him until dawn.

And based on the guide's odd behavior and the strange event, he wondered, though, if anything would be forthcoming.

«««—»»»

Parker's earlier assumption was dead on.

"Tell me what was out there. You know, don't you?"

Rijak shook his head, rummaging through one of several supply packs. The new day had arrived nearly an hour ago, and the two guides were focused on their duties while Parker questioned them. Liyar wouldn't even look him in the eye, but Parker would have sworn that he still saw fear in those green orbs. But fear of what?

Carlton was half-awake and gaining, shaking himself free of slumber. "Can't say I slept like a child, although I did dream of goose down pillows and a blazing hearth at my feet." His normally cheerful expression morphed into a look of curiosity. "Any problems? I hope the weather hasn't turned bad on us already."

Parker straightened, rocking back on his boot heels. "A most peculiar night, my friend. Most peculiar…"

Carlton was at full attention. "All right, what did I miss?"

"Ah, I really can't say, for the life of me. We heard the most astonishing sound last night, like nothing I've ever heard before. Although I don't know if *they* can make the same claim."

"What in the world was it?" Carlton leaned towards him, his brow raised in excitement.

"A weird cry, a keening of sorts. Extraordinary."

"And you didn't wake me?"

Parker gripped his arm. "I only heard it the one time. Well, twice, if you count while asleep…To be honest, I was so taken aback that I could barely move—I wanted to hear it again. And then it stopped. Nothing else for the remainder of the night, or early morning."

Carlton was clearly disappointed.

"Sorry," said Parker. "It had the oddest affect on me though. Don't think I've ever been quite that startled." It was a strong admission based on his varied experiences. "So I've been asking our good men here what it was. And…they have no answer."

"Strange indeed." Carlton stared at them both. Rijak nodded in greeting, but offered nothing else.

Parker tried again. "Rijak, you know everything that lives in these mountains. And we both *know* that it wasn't the sound of any common creature last night. Practically nothing can survive at this great height, and the few beasts that do are exceedingly rare." Here he hesitated. Rijak's face was impassive, but he gave Parker his full attention.

Lowering his voice, Parker continued. "Last night, the three of us heard something amazing. Could this have been the Kanchenjunga Demon?"

The small encampment was quiet, and even Liyar stopped what he was doing, recognizing the name. All eyes focused on Rijak for long moments before he replied.

"No."

<<<—>>>

For the rest of that morning the group explored the area immediately around their camp. The region was expansive, but the terrain wasn't very difficult. A fresh coating of snow had fallen overnight, but proved to be little challenge for their rugged gear. Parker conferred with Rijak on the direction, having the man lead them upwards and to either side of the camp as he searched for tracks. As the day grew long, Parker increasingly tried moving them towards the ridge, and they did so without resistance. It was only when they were nearing the huge crest when Rijak became nervous. "Sun has gone down, and we must go back."

Before them was a wicked peak which had to be crossed to reach the greater heights of the mountain. The topmost pinnacle was still invisible, shrouded by billowing clouds of snow, perpetually driven by the undying winds. It created a natural barrier for eyes which desired more, to penetrate the untamable cliffs and rock overhead. Parker felt the ominous presence of the summit hidden in the distance, and he was struck by a sense of awe that it could be so close, protected by its mantle of cold, rock, and restless elements. He wanted so badly to see…and *discover*, what secrets it held.

"Rijak, you know something that you're not telling me. I respect your beliefs, your folklore. We have the same stories in my land. Can you tell me why you won't go any higher? Is it because of what we heard last night?"

The guide hesitated, then spread his arms wide for emphasis. "What is the word, danger? Dangers? For us to go higher."

"What is it? What do you fear?"

The wind cried around them, flurries beginning to fall in thickening clumps.

"I do not know the word in your language."

"If it's money, I'll give you more. Just take us higher so we can search for whatever made that sound."

Rijak gently shook his head. "Getting late."

The two men turned about, heading downhill. They still had a decent hike ahead of them if they were to make the camp by nightfall. Parker walked close to Carlton, lowering his voice. "He's not telling us everything. He *knows* what we heard last night."

"Maybe he does. We've met enough superstitious folk in our travels, by all means. But they're not as hostile as some would be when treading on soft ground."

"Then we've indeed come as far as we can, led by these tight-lipped fellows."

"What do you propose? To head back already? We've come so far. I would at least like to stay here and search the area for another two or three days."

"That cry. It was like nothing I've ever heard before. I need to find out what it was."

Parker was silent for the remainder of their trek as they slowly descended, moving like ants crossing a desert wasteland of pure white.

«‹‹—››»

Despite his weariness, sleep was elusive for Parker that night. His dreams were disturbed by strange noises, terrible cries drifting down from the lofty peaks and valleys of the Himalayan mountains. He fidgeted in his sleep, tossing about, and finally woke up bathed in a cold perspiration. But this time the fire was stoked high and the two guides were...

Gone.

Carlton was staring at him, his eyes glazed over with excitement. And fear...

"Did you hear it? Parker?"

Shaking off his slumber Parker came to full alertness, trying to understand what had happened. "In my sleep, I heard the wailing again. Where have they gone?"

"They fled. Left us behind, I'm afraid."

"Did you see them leave?"

Carlton nodded. "The three of us were awakened by the cries. Rijak told me they were going back, and told me we must go. I refused."

"How long ago was that?"

"Only a few moments."

"And the sound?"

"We heard it twice."

Parker winced. "I'm not sure, but the sound that awakened me sounded even closer than last night." He locked stares with his companion, hesitating to ask his next question. "How far away *was* it?"

Carlton grabbed his arm.

"Nearly on *top* of us, man."

The fright was evident in his eyes.

Parker felt a shudder ripple across his skin. No wonder the guides had left in such haste...He looked at the walls of canvas protecting them from the harshness outside, the fierce elements, and perhaps something else. It appeared so fragile. And it was. But what did it separate them from? What manner of creature could survive the severity of this environment, even make it their home? For the first time he actually considered the possibility that what was out there might be far more than merely flesh and blood...

And then it happened.

A terrible wail, practically outside their tent. It was a voice of the wild incarnate—powerful and subtly mesmerizing. In the flash of a second, Parker heard tones in that dreadful sound which went beyond his understanding, suggestions of something possessing great strength, speaking in a language which surpassed the comprehension of men, a tongue which was in communion with treacherous cliffs, blinding storms, and gusting blizzards. Human ears would never be able to decipher such syllables as what they now listened to, a serenade both feral and intelligent, intent on its own purposes which had nothing in common with men and their trivial concerns. The *presence* Parker had felt earlier had been exposed and vocalized, and it was here with them now. It *knew* of their existence, and this reality came crashing down on him, heavier than an avalanche of ice and snow. Before, he'd been plagued with feelings of mild trepidation, nervous at the vastness of the mountains and its inescapable sense of isolation and permanence. Now, he was being held within its frigid clutches and he understood the frailty of his own life and the ease at which it could be snuffed out.

Carlton had passed into the next stage, twitching with fear, his face proclaiming how close he was to a total collapse of his senses. But Parker, although greatly disturbed, still retained his sanity, and a decent part of his courage. He would not entirely submit to the blackness. He snatched one of the lanterns, shouting to his companion. "Hold fast, I'll come back for you once I've seen this great thing which torments us."

His friend had entered into mild shock and merely sat there, mouth opened wide. Parker moved the flap, sweeping into the night, his light held firm. Outside was nothing but pitch, and his lamp cast an eerie glare across the snow-saturated landscape. Hesitating, he listened to the night, waiting to hear a telltale sign which would lead him on. Almost immediately it came from further up the mountain side, drawing him hither like a moth to the fateful flame. Part of him knew it was madness, but the urge to follow was primeval, and once he'd given in, there was no turning back. Sleep and weariness banished, he plunged ahead recklessly into the massive sheet of black and white, a fitting canvas duplicating his own polarized instincts. Time had no meaning here and all was perpetual darkness broken only by the disturbance of his meager flame. He went ever higher, moving straight upwards towards the heart of the mountain. The sound came down to him several times, like a beacon for lost souls. Perhaps he *was* lost at this point, lacking the concrete soundness of his normal reason, reacting solely on instinct. And if he was, there was nothing he could do to change it…

When he finally breached the uppermost part of the ridge, the night had run deep, the blackness surrounding him complete. His lantern illuminated the flakes swirling around him, and his breath came out in ragged gasps.

"Where are you now?" He cried out, falling to his knees. "What manner of beast have I pursued?" Parker envisioned the drawings he'd seen from witnesses of a tall, manlike beast, kin to the great lowland gorillas of the dense jungles. Would it finally be revealed to him now? Or had he wandered off on his own (or been led away), leaving the safer confines of the camp, placing himself in the most vulnerable of positions?

He waited, the wind exhaling from the higher reaches, smiting him with air colder than the grave.

And then he heard it…

The wailing echoed across the frozen plateau, whistling through crevices and circling around snow drifts. It was higher yet, but to his horror, it did not originate from the landscape before him.

But from overhead…

Impossible!

There was nothing there except an invisible sky and millions of stars, neither of which he could see. Above him? How could it have been from overhead? He stopped dead in his tracks, neck angled skyward. "What are you?" Parker screamed at the night, trying to find the source of the noise, answers to the questions which had led him so very far into these distant, untamable lands. He stumbled forward, moving precariously close to the ravine which yawned to the side. Confused, frightened, and frustrated, he demanded a reply, shouting into the night.

The wind died down and Parker held the lantern high, trying to pierce the mantle of black and white.

Then he froze as the sound bore down upon him, answering his plea. Something immense appeared, all scales and claws, its skin the color of mountain rock, a living incarnation of the mighty range and its inherent wildness, a creature borne on the pinnacle of the world, more legend than a physical entity.

Parker staggered, losing his footing, discovering too late that the ground beneath him had ceased to exist, and he felt himself falling, helpless to do anything but fixate on the image of the terrible thing which had finally revealed its presence to him.

In his last seconds, he found the answers he'd so desperately sought. There was no Yeti.

But there *were* dragons…

TWILIGHT'S EMBRACE

The Arizona landscape was fading into vagueness as long cracks of darkness slid over the desert valley, shrouding all within its wide cloak of twilight. The background horizon, painted brilliant orange and purple, was nearly gone, and the night promised to be clear and warm. And it could also prove to be unpredictable, especially for border patrols.

The small station buzzed with static from short wave radios, a pair of computer terminals flickering, the screens becoming snowy at times. Greg Laria stared at the bone-white clock on the wall, wondering when the call would come. And it would come, he knew...

Fixing the collar of his uniform he licked his dry lips, rubbing the day-old growth of stubble on his chin. He frowned in recollection of his last shave, where he'd noticed tiny flecks of gray for the first time. *Here comes forty. Time to buy a Porsche.*

Officer Reynolds sat next to him, absently tapping a pen on the edge of his desk. Sandy hair jutted out from beneath his cap, and his green eyes were narrow slits of concentration. Leader of the unit, his face was always impassionate, his mind and body alert. Greg stared at the older man with a look of mixed respect and curiosity.

He loves the chase. Lives for it.

Greg sipped at a cup of black coffee, scribbling on a small pad as Reynolds spoke.

"You'll be fine. Just remember—take absolutely nothing for granted out there. Keep your eyes open, and watch our backs. Damn cartel is pushing some heavy stuff up our way lately, as if we needed more problems. Nasty little bastards." Reynolds squinted in anger, and Greg nodded to his commander.

Reynolds continued, his voice sarcastic. "They sent you to a real hot bed—more than they told you, I'll bet. Thinned out our area while beefing up patrols to the east and west. Nice." He smirked, the closest expression he had to a smile. The radio crackled, and he quickly grabbed the receiver.

"Yeah, Reynolds."

Greg watched as the man nodded, jotting down notes on his scratch pad and tapping his monitor, which displayed a topographical map, the screen constantly changing as new positions were updated. After a brief conversation, he hung up the receiver and stood.

"Game time." He pointed with his index finger to a spot on the terminal. "That was Stewart's chopper. He's flying right about…here."

Greg moved closer. They were stationed just outside Tohono O'odam, which was a 5,000 square mile Indian reservation. Vast in size, it was also an extremely popular route for illegal immigrants crossing the border, as it shared scores of miles with Mexico.

A mixture of formidable resources were at the Border Patrol's disposal, including Line Watches which secured the international boundary itself, all-terrain vehicles, motorcycles, and helicopters. Surveillance in the air was also supported by blimps and planes as well. And thousands of agents patrolled on the ground. But it wasn't nearly enough to stop the endless flow of illegals crossing the border each year…

Reynolds continued. "Okay. We have one team right about here, and the group was spotted a few miles east, near Drun Road. They just dragged it yesterday, so it won't be hard to follow them."

"Are they on foot?" Greg stared at the screen, calculating the distance in his head.

"Nope. In a bus, if you can believe it."

"Bus? That's odd."

Reynolds laughed, low and humorless. "There's a lot of odd things going on down here. You never know what they'll do next." He reached down to the phone, pressing a red signal button. "Let's wait a minute until Badger comes."

The door behind them opened immediately as a tall officer walked in, his hair stark black, a bushy mustache nestled beneath a large, flat nose. He folded long arms over his angular frame. "A call?"

Reynolds nodded, showing him the positions on the screen. "We'll try to intersect them past here, force them into the Gill."

Greg remembered the landscape well enough from his orientation. The Gill was a deep gorge, which offered numerous hidden pockets for anyone who wanted to escape unfriendly eyes. It bordered the reservation, and consisted of empty desert for countless miles.

"How many vehicles?" Badger strapped on a sidearm as he questioned his superior.

"Stewart spotted only one."

"Hmm. No *coyote* then."

Greg was silent, listening to the short remarks. The term *coyote* referred to 'people smugglers,' guides who would often lead migrants to their death, stranding them in the middle of the desert. A cold and dangerous breed, lacking any conscience.

"Let's move quick." Reynolds grabbed a backpack filled with supplies and ammunition. He gave Greg a hard look. "Looks like your first night should be pretty interesting."

The three men left the building as they hurried to the garage.

«‹‹—›››

A pair of SUVs carrying the three men rumbled across the desert plains, churning up dust clouds in their wake. Lizards and hares scurried out of the way, disappearing into the scrub brush and rocks.

Greg sat in the passenger seat with a map in his hand while Badger drove in the first vehicle. An infrared scope hung loosely about Greg's neck, and he stared at the road before him which was illuminated by the powerful cutting lights. The vehicle was fitted with its own terminal and GPS module, and it was Greg's task to constantly monitor their position, at times communicating with Reynolds who followed behind, and keeping in touch with another patrol pursuing from further east.

"Is this the usual setup, trailing them into the gorge with another unit waiting at the far end?" Greg adjusted the brightness knob on the monitor.

"Yeah." Badger never took his eyes off the road ahead.

"Chopper out there?"

"Probably won't need one." Badger shook his head.

"Oh?" Greg looked at him curiously.

The other man paused for a moment before responding. "They don't always come *out* of the Gill."

"But you don't think they have a *coyote* leading them—or do you?"

"Hmm, maybe. I don't know. It's just that some weird things happen down there. Abandoned trucks, damaged equipment, and no Mexicans in sight."

Greg pursued his questioning. "They walk on foot to escape? Leave their vehicle? That's crazy. There's nothing but sand for a hundred miles in all directions. A man would have to be a fool to try it on foot out here."

Badger snorted. "A fool, maybe...or desperate."

Greg heard something strange in his tone, and wanted to know what else the man knew. "I guess they're all desperate in a sense, crossing illegally—some of them never making it."

Badger shot him a quick glance. "A lot of them die out here. Do you have any idea how many?"

"Several hundred last year alone were reported."

"Right. Reported..."

"So, there's more. They'll never find them all." Greg looked outside as the ground became rockier.

"Try a *lot* more." Badger's voice was low.

Greg raised his eyebrows. "As in...?"

"Over a thousand, many of them right around our perimeter."

Greg let out a low whistle, then sat there in silence for a while. "And you know this for a fact? But what's happening to them?"

Badger replied, his face dark. "Here's what I know." He paused. "There have been signs of violence, trucks and vans broken into, glass smashed. And blood everywhere..."

He quietly stared at the dusty road before them. "Something's killing them around the reservation, especially in the Gill."

《《——》》

It was approaching midnight when both vehicles stopped, Greg and Badger picking up the fresh trail along Drun Road. Reynolds left his truck and walked towards the others, chattering into his hand radio for several moments. He ended the brief conversation, engaging his own men.

"They'll move in from the east, make sure the group doesn't veer off. The tracks are clean—they didn't even try to brush anything out."

Badger peered ahead. "In a hurry, as usual. But do they know what's out there?"

Greg followed his gaze. "The question is do *we* know?"

Reynolds tilted his head, first to Greg, then Badger. "Hmm, you told him about our little secret then." It was a statement.

"Just that there are a lot of illegals missing out here. Unexplained disappearances. I guess he'll find out soon enough for himself." Badger shrugged.

"All right. Let's get on with it." Reynolds walked back to his truck, ignoring Greg's questioning stare.

«‹‹—›››

They rumbled along through the night in their vehicles, and had traveled a few miles when a large shape loomed unexpectedly before them. It was the bus…Badger slammed the break, bringing their truck to an abrupt halt. He motioned to Greg, both men grabbing their weapons.

"Radio our position. Reynolds will circle around and throw us some more light."

Greg called in to the other group, and they waited in silence as Reynolds drove to their right, strategically casting his own headlights and adding to the visibility. The landscape looked eerie, dust lifting from the desert ground, and Greg couldn't help feeling nervous. Moments later, they heard the static of a loudspeaker, as Reynolds identified their presence and office, and demanded for the illegals to come out with hands held up. Nothing happened for several long seconds, and even Badger looked tense, absently tapping his weapon.

"I don't like this; I've seen it before. They're either holding out on us, carrying some expensive payload, or…"

Reynolds jumped out of his truck, rifle pointed forward. He barked orders into the night, and Badger gestured for Greg to follow his lead.

"Can't trust these bastards—keep a sharp eye, just in case they try to circle around us. I don't think they knew we were coming though." Badger eased himself forward, Greg beside him, both men scanning the entire area.

The desert was deathly quiet, the wind hushed. High clouds crested overhead, chasing the nearly-full moon, which cast an argent glow over the sand and making it shimmer. Greg felt the solitude press in on him—the stagnant air, the endless hills of barren rock, the miles of desert separating them from even the smallest, most outlying town. They were far away from comfort and familiarity—very far away—playing a dangerous game with unpredictable people…

The bus was smoking. The engine hood had been pulled up, and it appeared the vehicle had suffered from a broken radiator hose. A disaster for someone in their precarious situation, in the middle of a vast wilderness. Reynolds trotted towards them.

"No one in sight. Let's move in."

As they neared the bus, they saw that it was rusted and soiled from the harsh weather, the surface paint peeling off and impossible for them to even guess at the original color.

"What a piece of…" Badger halted before he could finish. There was broken glass everywhere. Great shards lay in piles before several of the windows. And worse yet. There were crimson stains on the desert sand.

"Stay alert," Reynolds whispered to his men, and they scanned the scene nervously. "Badger, take the watch. I'll lead, Greg right behind me. Make sure you see what you're shooting at—if it comes down to that. Hate to see you plug a hole in some poor lady."

Greg frowned at the remark. "Try my best…sir."

Badger grunted next to him, backing up and moving to the front of the stranded vehicle.

The two men crept towards the door which was wide open. The inside was dark, and Reynolds held his flashlight ready, splashing his beam in a sweeping arc. Nothing moved, and Greg felt a growing sense of dread. Where were all the people?

Reynolds stepped into the bus, finger on the trigger of his rifle. Badger whistled over to him, peering through an infrared scope. "Looks deserted. Careful, you never know."

Reynolds hesitated for a moment before going inside, Greg immediately following on his heels. The interior was empty except for a number of sacks which probably held clothing and other essential items from the illegals. A pair of water coolers lay on their side, and the place was in an upheaval. Glass covered the worn seats, which were ripped apart and unsteady. Half of the windows were shattered, and the emergency exit in the back was locked. And blood was splattered all over—against the remaining windows, on the seats, and covering the floor.

"What the hell happened here?" Greg was shocked by the scene, the cold hand of fear creeping along his back.

Reynolds only shook his head, pulling out his radio. "Reporting, this is Reynolds with Squire Unit." He hesitated, remembering their coordinates. "Um…and we've found the bus, it's abandoned. No one around. Looks like another C-16, a real mess. Over."

The receiving contact on the other end quickly answered, following through with orders, and Reynolds sighed.

"Let's pull back, the boys will pick up this junker tomorrow. Time to head out."

Greg looked at him in surprise. "That's it? What about the Mexicans? Aren't we even going to look for them? And all this blood. What *happened* here…"

The officer cut him off. "I don't know, but I have my orders. Someone else takes over from here. It's not our job anymore." He pointed to the door.

In disbelief, Greg retreated, stepping out again into the night. Badger was alert, positioning himself to maximize his view of the lighting, scanning their surroundings. "Another one?"

"Yeah." Reynolds shouldered his weapon, the man obviously eager to leave the bus behind.

"Now wait a second." Greg held up a hand. "Somebody please tell me what's going on here, and why no one seems concerned that a bunch of illegals were ambushed and slaughtered."

"I'm following *orders.*" Reynolds frowned at him with narrow eyes. "And I don't know what's going on either, except that we have to leave, and now. Whoever killed them might still be around."

"So you admit they were killed then…and what else?"

"You're coming dangerously close to insubordination. I'll tell you more when we return."

"But people are dead out here," Greg pleaded with him.

Reynolds sighed, and looked genuinely upset. "I know. I'll tell you real quick. We think it's the local Indians, maybe some cult or something. Pissed off at the Mexicans, or whatever reason, I don't know…But central is well aware of what's been happening, and strictly forbids us to go searching for any survivors when it does happen. They're handling it. Now let's *go.*"

They started to walk away when a low cry came from the bus.

Snatching their weapons high, all three of them pivoted, facing the vehicle. Sobbing came from somewhere nearby, and Badger hissed. "Someone's alive."

Reynolds pursed his lips. "It was empty, and you checked the other side."

"Wait," snapped Greg. "Underneath."

Reynolds moved in, flashing his light beneath the bus. "It's a boy, hiding behind the front wheel." He moved closer, sticking one hand in front, gently pulling out a dark-haired youth, dirty with tattered clothes, maybe twelve years old. The child was terrified, trembling with eyes blinking frantically.

"He's in shock." Greg helped Reynolds with the youth, while Badger stayed on guard. "We need to get some blankets and give him water." They pulled him out, but as soon as they did, he unexpectedly broke from their grip and dashed towards the front door. Reynolds closed his hand on empty air in surprise, and Greg was taken totally by surprise.

"Damn…" Reynolds swore, standing there in frustration.

"We can't just leave him out here." Greg hurried after the boy, Reynolds still cursing, but following behind. They watched as the door slammed shut, and Greg tried forcing it open.

"I'll get the back. Kick it in awhile." Reynolds raced along the side of the bus, muttering to himself.

《《——》》

Greg pressed in on the door, but it failed to budge. The kid was quick, in shock or not. And his eyes—he'd been terrified. But by what?

Shouts from the back echoed towards him, and Reynolds yelled for the boy to open. Greg stood back, then took a running leap, kicking furiously at the door, leaving a shallow depression. He clamped down on his teeth, feeling the pain even through his tough boots. Nice bruise there tomorrow, he thought. Yeah, well.

He shoved the door using his shoulder and it buckled inwards. Moving swiftly he entered, flicking on his flashlight and looking for the youth. He wasn't hard to find. The boy was huddled in the middle of the vehicle, rambling words in Spanish. Reynolds had grown impatient, kicking in the emergency door, looking determined not to let the kid escape again. They both approached, but it appeared as if the boy wasn't going to resist.

"No tricks this time, kid. Let's get you out of here." Reynolds put away his light and flung his rifle over one shoulder, stooping to pick up the boy, who was shaking in fear.

"It's all right," whispered Greg. "You'll be safe now."

From outside they heard Badger whistle, then his face appeared at a broken window. "What's taking you so long? It's only one skinny kid."

"Keep alert, Badger." Reynolds was angry that the man hadn't listened. "Cover the perimeter...now!" Badger gave a sheepish look and turned around.

At that moment, the strangest noise broke through the night, and the boy's eyes spread wide in horror. "Eh, eh!" He choked the words, and the men looked around in confusion. To Greg, it sounded like the droning of a swarm of insects—a low buzzing, but steady, the tone grating his ears.

A scream shredded the night and they heard gunshots outside.

Greg caught a glimpse of Badger's silhouette through the cracked glass, and to his shock a dark form seemed to swoop from the sky, smashing into the man and lifting him up in the air. It happened so quickly that he thought he'd imagined the whole thing.

But Badger had disappeared...

Reynolds was frozen, still holding the boy, who clutched at him, pounding away at his chest to release him.

"What the hell was that!" Greg stared outside in amazement and shock, slowly lifting his weapon. Reynolds only shook his head, silent.

"Something flew from the sky...and took Badger. Is this happening? Reynolds!"

For one terrible moment Greg thought his commander had lost his senses and would be incapable of action. But the man snapped his head around, swearing, and hurried to the front of the bus, carrying the boy. "Move! Whatever that thing was, it'll be back soon."

Greg didn't need to question the order, and he followed Reynolds down the short steps, jumping out and landing on the soft desert sand. The leader scanned the area, then sped towards his truck. Greg then noticed that the floodlights on the first truck were flickering, and he shouted to Reynolds. "The battery must be going! I'm coming with you." Reynolds gave a quick nod of approval as he opened the front door, pushing the boy inside first. Greg jumped in the backseat, never lowering his weapon.

"I'm calling for help. I don't know what it was, but that thing's responsible for killing all the illegals." Reynolds turned on the ignition, at the same time signaling on the radio.

"Let's get out of here first." Greg looked nervously outside, where the light was dimming as the first truck's battery continued to drain.

Reynolds reversed the vehicle, speaking into the receiver at the same time. "Badger is gone—something killed him. Came from out of the sky…" He faltered for a moment, then continued, gasping for breath.

"Hey—hang in there." Greg saw the fright reflected in Reynolds' eyes, the sweat pouring down the man's brow. The boy mumbled something in his own language—the same word, over and over again. Greg leaned forward, listening intently.

Reynolds chattered into the receiver, looking increasingly frustrated. He suddenly slammed down the unit, halting the vehicle.

"What—what's wrong?" Greg grabbed the man's shoulder.

The officer looked disgusted. "They ordered us to stay exactly where we are. Not to move."

They locked gazes in silence.

"You've got to be kidding…" Greg finally broke, stunned. "Didn't they believe you?"

Reynolds stared outside, checking the lock on his door. The boy continued rambling, and Greg thought he could make out a single word. "What's he mumbling? Wait, I know. He's saying…" He paused, chills claiming his skin.

"Chupacabra."

Reynolds whispered softly, his voice quaking. "I've heard of it—a Mexican legend. Sort of like the Jersey Devil, or something like that. I always thought it was a bunch of crap. But right now, I don't know what to think." Reynolds eased the truck into motion, pulling down the road. "And we're not staying to find out…"

"Do you think they know about this thing then?" Greg's mind churned as a dreadful idea spread outward, seeping into his heart and poisoning his hope. "And they wanted us to stay? I don't like this—not at all!"

The light cut a path through the empty desert, fear and despair hiding behind every clump of boulders, the night sky sheltering death itself in the form of the unspeakable entity which had taken Badger. Greg kept shaking his head as the hideous notion came to fruition, and for one terrible moment he was unable to speak. He finally swallowed, finding the words once again.

"If they *do* know, then maybe they're manipulating things."

Reynolds stared at him through the rearview window.

Greg continued, his voice uncertain. "You said the surrounding area had received additional agents, deployed in greater numbers on either side of the reservation. But our precinct—near the Gill—has been reduced."

"What are you getting at?" Reynolds croaked the words.

"They're pushing the illegals to move through this way. Because they know what's waiting here. Listen…systematic genocide, without bloodying their own hands."

The other man slammed his hand on the steering wheel. "That's outrageous. Do you know what you're saying?" Reynolds stared coldly at him.

Greg nodded defiantly. "Yeah, I do. This thing—they're using it to reduce the flow of migrants. A ruthless, invisible killer, leaving no trace, except for dead Mexicans. Easy enough to forget about some runaway illegals. Who would believe that a monster is acting as the ultimate border deterrent? Think about it…"

Both men were silent as they drove slowly along the road.

After a while, Reynolds spoke. "I don't believe it, but I saw that creature, or something I can't explain. Whatever it is, it's real—and extremely dangerous."

"But where does that leave us?" Greg looked outside. "Why did they want us to stay?" The same horrible thought lingered in both their minds. Neither man wanted to speak the grisly words.

The boy sobbed. His head was folded beneath his arms. *"Chupacabra."*

It was like a verdict of undeniable truth, terrible and powerful. Greg leaned forward, whispering to Reynolds. "We know what's out here—and that makes *us* dangerous. I have a really bad feeling about this." He paused for a second. "The lights," he snapped.

Reynolds halted the vehicle and turned off the beams. "What next?"

"Let's look outside once."

Cautiously, they left the truck, holding their weapons tightly. The sky overhead was clear, and they searched the night for any sign of the creature. Greg pointed to the north. "Look. I didn't think it would take very long."

Two pairs of lights could be seen in the distance. Helicopters. They were bearing down on the area they'd just left. A few seconds later, an explosion ripped across the landscape, startling both men.

"Rotten bastards…" Reynolds spat. "They don't want anyone to know their ugly little secret." The officer had recovered somewhat, rage taking over his fear. It was a grim thought. They were exiles themselves now, on the run from their own government.

"It might be a good idea to split up." Reynolds remained staring at the horizon, fingering his weapon. "Come morning, they'll be picking apart this region."

Greg answered. "Sooner. They have infrared cameras on their choppers, and they might notice our tracks going back. And they already know two vehicles were dispatched…" The men locked gazes. Greg looked inside the truck but the boy was motionless, overcome by exhaustion and fright.

Reynolds nodded. "Well, there's the three-wheeler in the back, plenty of extra water and supplies for us both, enough weapons for sure. Although if *that* becomes necessary, you're as good as dead anyway…"

"Okay, I'll unload it." Greg ran around to the back, unfastening the hatch and lowering the vehicle. Large and sturdy, it was capable of traveling in extreme conditions, fitted with a spare gas tank. He packed on his weapon and supplies, while Reynolds guarded against the approach of anything. The boy lifted his head and quietly opened the door, walking towards Greg.

"Feeling better?" Greg noticed the youth standing there, and smiled at him.

"Took a liking to you I guess." Reynolds waited near the front of the truck. "The helicopters are grounded, or else we would have seen some light. Unless they're hunting us now…"

Greg didn't like *that* train of thought. He mounted the vehicle, ready to leave. The boy touched his arm, but Greg gently shook his head. "No, you'll be safer in the truck." But the boy was persistent. Greg looked hopelessly at Reynolds, who shrugged.

"There's room for two. I can't be watching him every step of the way, I have my own back to guard."

Greg smiled. "All right, hop in my little *Amigo.*" He helped the boy up, revving the engine. "Good luck, Reynolds," he waved.

"See you in Mexico." The officer shot him a mocking salute, and Greg's face drained of color at what he saw.

Perched on top of the truck was a nightmare.

The thing was charcoal black, leathered wings folded across its scaled back. The face was hideous, the features exaggerated and monstrous. Gaping fangs hung over huge, rubbery lips. All four appendages ended in massive, disproportionately large claws. And the terrible eyes gleamed the color of cold ashes, promising death.

The droning issued forth from its gaping mouth, and it lunged forward. Fate alone chose Greg to survive that second encounter—nothing else. With incredible speed and fury it was on Reynolds before he had a chance to even scream. It crushed the man's head where he stood and flew off with him into the shadows. It happened so quickly that Greg failed to even move. His body simply could not react in such a short amount of time.

The boy was mute, nothing left inside for him to scream, cry, speak, and maybe not even think…They'd seen the creature of legend, and had been marked by it. Whatever time they had left was now borrowed.

Greg cranked the three-wheeler and they roared off into the desert, fleeing from nightmares into the arms of nightmares. The boy was held tightly in another seat belt, and the rush of air felt cold and clammy on Greg's arms and back. He did the only thing left for him to do, and that was to go forward as fast as possible, escape from the hideous thing that waited behind and perhaps continued to hunt them.

Maybe it would abandon the two when they left the Gill. But surely the government wouldn't.

Greg focused on the desert terrain, ignoring the quiet beauty and wonder passing them by. Ignoring the watchful glare of the moon casting its lunar magnificence below. Ignoring everything in the world, except for one terrible thought. A question for which he didn't have an answer, and didn't really want to find out. Greg couldn't decide which one was worse.

The real monsters or the human ones…

PURGATORY CALLING

Gunfire in the distance...mortar shells exploding, tree branches shattering in the murky twilight of the swampy lowland. The smells of war engulf him—sweat, oiled steel, fire. Mindless terror threatens to overwhelm him, and he pauses, heart raging inside his weary chest. He looks to his right. Marty is still with him, and further off, the silhouettes of two more in his platoon, vague manlike suggestions, crouching in the primeval hell of the violated jungle.

"Steve? Where's Steve..."

He shakes his head in confusion, looking to his left, but there is no sign of the younger man, instead only haze and the unrelenting undergrowth.

"He was right there a minute ago. Right there!"

His voice raises in fear, carrying over to the others of the group, their numbers severely diminished by a disastrous surprise attack from the Viet Cong. Their commander dead, only these few terrified men remain, desperately trying to escape the clutches of death once more, which can take many forms—trip wire, a grenade flash, strafing close-range machine gun fire, or a stray mortar shell.

Something shrieks overhead and he finds himself reflexively crashing to the ground as a tremendous explosion sends them all diving for cover.

Long, terrible moments pass and he finally opens his eyes, blinking madly, wondering if he's still alive. The jungle is strangely silent...Fate has spared him again, but how many more times will he emerge unscathed until his face is drawn on the card of doom?

It's unnatural, the quiet.

Maybe the entire world has been torn apart, he thinks. Ravished by the hatred and violence of men. And he would gladly welcome it…

At first it appears he's alone, and dread seizes his heart with the possibility of isolation in that vast and perilous jungle. Trembling, he looks around. Marty's body lays beneath the cover of a moss-eaten log, but he's moving. Is he all right? He glances over to his left, but there is still no sign of Steve. It's as if the jungle has opened up and swallowed him whole.

And then, the most remarkable thing happens. There is the sound of something very far off, a man shouting, but the words are muffled. Animals howl, and the jungle is disturbed by movement. The Viet Cong? Why would they make such obvious noise?

Immediately, he knows this to be untrue. Breathing deeply, tasting bile in his throat, he's overcome by a feeling of utter terror, although he doesn't know why. There is another blast echoing through the jungle, a strange sound but not gunfire, and then no more…

Kyle rubbed a callused hand across his brow.

"Tired?"

"No. Bad memories. Flashbacks, I guess."

"Damn." Marty swore, standing up and leaning on the cedar rail of the deck. "I have 'em all the time. Can't sleep, sometimes I just sit up at night, staring at the TV. Or the wall…What the hell were we *doing* over there?"

"I ask myself that one every day." Kyle stood as well, drinking from a bottle of Coors. He glanced at Marty's wide shoulders. The guy looked like he could still plug his way through a horde of defensive backs like a wild bull. His hair was shoulder length, tied into a ponytail with a red bandanna. Child of the sixties, victim of the seventies…

Both men stared at the countryside. They stood on the back deck of Kyle's log cabin which was nestled deeply in a valley between low foothills on the threshold of the Pocono Mountains. Basically a cozy hunter's lodge, it was isolated, surrounded by nothing but dense forest for scores of miles. If Pennsylvania had a frontier, this was it. And it was impressive.

"Beautiful place, man. But I don't know if I like it better than in the city. Less reminders there." Marty fastened a button on his brown flannel shirt against the autumn chill. Nightfall was descending after a spectacular sunset. The last brilliant orange rays had sunk behind them into the woods a while ago, the sky a dream of clear blue. Perfection, if it existed. Stars glittered overhead, and they breathed the clean air. Pine, the perfume of late-blooming flowers, the scent of burning wood from inside—all normal and pleasant smells one could expect on the last day of October.

"Hey, it's Halloween, " Marty sighed. "Just remembered that…Judy and the kid will be out tonight, I guess. Or last night, maybe. Mischief night or whatever they call it. When I was a kid, man, we terrorized the neighborhood. Things have changed though. They don't go for any of that crap anymore. It's a shame, really…" His voice drifted off, the lines on his forehead creasing in a deep frown. "Times change."

"Not everything." Kyle looked over at his friend. "All Hallow's Eve—that's when our platoon got ambushed from those bastards. Took Sterner down, most of the others. I'll never forget it." His words bitter, he felt his throat constrict, the wings of anxiety threatening to swoop over him.

"Sonofabitch…yeah, I didn't forget. Thought if I didn't talk about it, things would get easier." Marty held his own bottle tightly within his huge grip before raising it to his mouth.

"It doesn't though. I don't think it ever will." Kyle stared at the forest, his gray eyes unfocused. The memories always came—sometimes because he wanted them to, and other times when he didn't. Vivid and terrible, they would not be denied. Drugs, therapy, booze, nothing helped. Like the pictures of an endless film looping over and over, the memories were imprinted within his mind's eye, the screams of dying men a litany of horror, the faces of the dead a silent testament to the madness and evil of war. They couldn't be refused. Terrible, but undeniably the reality of his past. And Kyle thought that was the problem with many of the other vets—they tried to drown out the images instead of accepting them for what they were. He felt repression was the ultimate downfall. One's heart and conscience could take in only so much pain without release…

Crickets chirped from the high grass and bushes, and Kyle felt his mood soften a bit. Understanding. That's what he'd spent most of the past two decades trying to do—understand the events which had so profoundly shaken him, and eventually remade him into the man he was today. Acceptance…at least to some degree. But too many unanswered questions remained.

"The night Steve disappeared. I'll go to my grave wondering what the hell happened to him. Vanished into thin air…"

"I know. I can't remember much, that mortar shell took me out for a while. Lost half my hearing from that bad boy." Marty tried to grin, but the gesture was empty, and he knew it.

Kyle looked skyward as a nearly-full moon crested the forested ridge. "I was the only one with half a wit left. Somehow, I came to right away. Or never got knocked out. I just don't *know.*"

"Man, you gotta' let it go. There's nothing you could have done. None of us know what happened to the guy."

Kyle smashed his bottle onto the deck, feeling a rising wave of fury. "Damn! He was just a kid! He didn't know a thing, it wasn't his fault." He scorched Marty with a look of hostility, and his friend flinched at the pain etched in Kyle's face, and it went much deeper…

"Crazy. Everyone was nuts, you know? Bunch of kids and dopeheads, killing someone we didn't know, for something we had no business in messin' with…" He looked at his boots, not wanting to see anymore of Kyle's face.

After a few seconds, the uncertainty passed. Kyle felt the outrage seep away, leaving only an emptiness in the pit of his stomach, a pang almost like hunger that couldn't be quenched. An overwhelming sense of sadness crushed down on him and the tears flowed. They were impotent though, unable to do anything but merely dampen the internal fire which burned inside—one which could materialize again at any time.

Marty patted him on the arm.

Kyle sighed, letting the cool moisture of his tears trickle down onto his lips and mouth. "I can't *imagine* what he felt. Killing that family. But it wasn't his fault…"

"Yeah, no one ever blamed him either. That happened all the time over there. It was hell."

Kyle nodded—not in response to his friend's remarks, but to the image in his head—the smoking ruin of a tribal hut, the stricken look on Steve's boyish face as he emerged, his skin pale white beneath the boiling orange of the unforgiving Asian sun. Scattered gunfire, a trap set in place for the Americans. Confusion. And Steve had mistakenly thought the Viet Cong had been in the last hut in that small forsaken village. Acted upon fear and instinct.

With catastrophic results…

Marty spoke again. "Maybe he got lost, or did himself in. The guilt..." He didn't care to finish.

"No." Kyle shook his head savagely. "Not lost. He was *right* with us. Steve left on his own. Why? I don't know. Maybe he did kill himself, but not then. We would've heard the shot."

Marty shrugged, his face neutral.

Kyle looked up, staring into the distance. "But that shout, and the other noises. Nothing like I heard before in that whole stinkin' place. It was...weird."

"Nam' messed us all up. You know that. You're killin' yourself, trying to figure it all out, Kyle. You gotta' stop it, man. Gotta' stop it..."

Marty moved away from the rail, stooping to pick up pieces of broken glass.

"I'll get it..." Kyle started, but the other man waved him off.

"Grab another beer—one for me, too. Hey, it's your cabin. Don't want to be just a freeloader."

"You're never that, you big ass." Kyle snapped at his friend. "Don't even go there..."

After a few moments the glass had all been picked up, and the men eased down onto the bottom steps leading into the yard. Kyle stood on the grass, leaning against the trellis which enclosed the area beneath the deck. The cabin and yard were illuminated in a sheen of silver, and both men admired the tranquility of their surroundings. But Kyle was uneasy. Thinking about Steve and his disappearance always made him feel bad. There was a terrible weight on his own conscience, and he experienced a sense of hopelessness and despair for the man. If only he could somehow lift the burden of guilt and purge it away—for both of them. It was dangerous to wander along that path—he could lose himself in that nightmare, and he knew it. But he still couldn't overcome the feeling despite the risk.

"Busy day tomorrow," Marty rumbled, trying to lighten the mood, although Kyle heard the weariness in his friend's voice. "Late season trout fishing, knocking off some target practice, splitting a few cords. *That* chore I could pass on..."

Kyle nodded, staring down at the large pile of kindling stacked neatly along the far side of the deck. Winter was coming, the dark season. November eagerly waited, with its threat of snow and cold weather. The holidays were coming as well. But they did little for him anymore. Just added to his general sense of helplessness. Depression, yeah, but not just that, although he did wonder if he really was border-line suicidal. But no, he'd never felt the urge to go that route. To him that wasn't the answer, and never would be…

He could see his own breath now. Cool vapor from his mouth. The air was brisk, but clean. Good for breathing and thinking. Comforted by the presence of his old friend, Kyle tried to relax. Tried to let the alcohol flow through his veins and ease the anxiety. I can't just dwell on the past all the time, he chided himself. Try to live for once—really live. Things weren't all that bad for him.

It was true. Money, friends, security, his health—at least his *physical* health, although his emotional and mental well-being were at times suspect. But he'd been through all the tests and therapy sessions over the years. Under his circumstances, he was pretty normal, and better than many, he was told. So most of these things—if not all—were in place.

And still the past continued to haunt him…

"Beautiful night there, partner." Marty pointed upwards, and walked away from the deck, his arms spread wide. "You know, it's easy to forget all this, living in the 'burbs."

"That's why I'm up here a lot. More and more, these days." Kyle shuffled aimlessly across the grass. "Nature seems to call. It's almost a compulsion."

"What do you mean? Maybe you'd rather avoid people? I can see that."

Kyle turned to his friend. "I don't really know." He shrugged. "But I feel *drawn* here, sometimes. Especially when I think about Steve. And this time of year most of all."

"Hmm. Nothing strange there. Except you need to let go a little—or more."

"But I can't deny my *own* guilt." Kyle's face turned severe. Marty appeared ready to speak but stopped, letting Kyle release his frustration. "Steve was convinced the Viet Cong were in that hut, but I didn't try to stop him either. My hands are just as bloody."

Now Marty interjected. "C'mon, enough of this guilt crap…"

"No."

Kyle cut him off, but this time, not in anger, only in sadness. "No." His voice softened. "When he insisted, I had a chance to hold him back.

We were on the far side, with Higgins and Brigg. I remember the look he gave me, man. His eyes were angry, and scared, and nuts, I don't know…"

There was a long pause.

"But by my *inaction*, I helped him slaughter those poor villagers. And I can't wipe away the guilt, no matter what I say or do…"

Kyle bowed his head while Marty looked on helplessly. When Kyle lifted his neck, he knew that his friend wondered if he were about to do something terrible. And was he? Could he finally be that desperate after all the long years?

They locked eyes for well over a minute and the world seemed to stand still. The forest grew hushed, and Kyle trembled with fear. The night leaned down on them—watching, waiting, and listening.

But the look on Marty's face was far worse than any reaction to what Kyle might have done…The man's eyes went wide with fright, and Kyle shuddered. Marty had the look of someone scared to the very bone. At first Kyle thought he was staring at him, but no, his eyes were fixed on something *behind* him.

And that was a horrifying thought…

What did he see?

Kyle turned slowly, awkwardly, in the direction which had so entranced his companion. Towards the end of the yard, where the trees encroached, their wide trunks looming in the distance like ancient behemoths, guarding the primeval forest.

He faced the darkness, eyes squinting in disbelief…

…as a figure emerged from the black maw of the wilderness.

It appeared to be a man.

Closer, the person came, directly for them.

What? Out here?

Who could possibly be coming? No one lived for countless miles in any direction.

Maybe a hunter, lost and disoriented? It was definitely a man, judging from their height and build. But there was obviously something wrong, and he walked as if crushed beneath a weight, at times slumping forward, moving uncertainly to either side.

Marty stepped forward, joining his friend, and Kyle glanced at his face. His skin was deathly white—he was terrified. Seeing Marty's fear only increased his own consternation, and soon he felt cold, but not from the air. They both stared at the intruder, neither one of them willing—or able—to speak.

The man was only yards away, his face shrouded in shadows, the features indiscernible. The appearance of this wanderer was so absolutely *strange*, as if the deep vastnesses of the forest had opened up, spewing forth this unknown being, his purpose cloaked in secrecy. The man stopped, and Kyle felt Marty grip his shoulder, hard enough to be painful, but he ignored the sensation.

All three of them waited. For something…Anything.

The following silence was dreadful. The entire landscape was hushed, the hills and trees conceding mute attention to the trio of shadows standing motionless beneath the glistening veil of the rising moon. The quiet was unbearable.

But even more terrible were the soft, anguished words which now issued forth from the stranger's lips.

"It's me."

Kyle felt his knees bend, on the verge of collapse. The forest closed in on him.

Marty tried to talk, but nothing intelligible came out, his throat too constricted for anything but garbled noises. He sounded pathetically like a young or ignorant child, unable to form proper letters.

Neither one of them *dared* respond as they shared the same unspoken thought. Kyle had somehow known the identity of the stranger who now stood before them. He knew, and Marty knew. Although it was quite impossible.

Across the years, wading through dark waters of innumerable night-mares, and now emerging from the woods behind Kyle's cabin, it was *him*.

"Steve…"

Marty sobbed like a frightened infant, but Kyle only stood aghast, mouth open wide in shock and terror. He told himself that his mind had finally plunged over the abyss, and he was ready to accept the embrace of madness, perhaps even welcoming its icy touch. It was far easier to believe this explanation than the *other* possibility…

That Steve had returned. Had found his companions from that black and dreadful place of death and chaos. The battlefield which had so effectively and completely raped them of their innocence. A reunion of lost, young, unwilling warriors, who had been shipped off to an exotic and hostile land far from the warm, familiar trappings of their own homes. All their youthful expectations had been violated, transformed forever. Innocent no longer...

The man stumbled forward. His clothing was tattered, ripped and soiled almost beyond description. Almost...

But Kyle recognized the old uniform. It was the same one which he'd worn on that last fateful day. The last time they'd all been together. And now—impossibly—they were all together again.

"How? What..." Kyle tried to form the proper questions, but his mind simply couldn't react. He gestured absently, his limbs tingling as if asleep. Sweat poured from his brow, the moisture just one more unpleasant sensation along with all the others. Should he laugh? Cry? Scream? Marty was stricken beside him, the bearish man stripped of his usual confidence, laid bare and vulnerable.

"The guilt. I couldn't live with the guilt."

Kyle blinked several times, nearly panting in fear, but the grim figure before him remained. "You're dead?" He didn't know if it was a question or a statement, but there was no way this was their former companion, miraculously appearing on his very doorstep. He looked unnatural, although there was nothing in particular he could single out, except for the man's very *presence* itself. A spirit? Fantastic it seemed, but no worse than anything else at this moment. Either that, or madness. But which one did he prefer?

"I can't stay. He'll be calling me back."

Kyle felt ice in his blood at the mention of someone else. Who could he possibly mean? Were there more of these dreadful phantoms waiting in the trees? A company of the dead?

"Why did you come...?"

Part of him wanted so badly to hear the answer, and another part of him prayed there would be no answer forthcoming. The stranger turned, as if listening. They all waited, and listened. The solitude and terror reached out from the shadows and claimed them as victims.

And then they heard it...

In the distance, harsh yells. It sounded like the braying of dogs. Dogs? Then, without warning, a tremendous thundering, as of a horn bellowing in the night, the notes slicing through the forest, powerful and ominous. Kyle had a sense of terrible strangeness, something completely untamed and utterly unknown to men. The noise grew louder, closer, and the man claiming to be Steve started back towards the trees. He angled his neck, staring directly at Kyle. In place of eyes, there was only a black void.

"Release your guilt. I couldn't."

With that, he continued moving, steadily gaining speed until he was nearly running straight for the deep woods, his feet seeming to *glide* across the grass. Marty gasped, inhaling huge gulps of air while holding his chest. Kyle felt a new surge of helplessness assault him, and he screamed at the retreating figure. "No! You can't leave me again!"

His words were left unanswered, and he started following after his lost companion. It was too much for Marty and he tried to stop him. "Kyle," he choked. "No…" But his friend was already several yards away and moving quickly. Steve was now at the forest eaves, vanishing into blackness as the great horn sounded again, the entire countryside seeming to hunker down beneath its fell call.

Kyle never stopped, feeling an urgency not to lose his old comrade a second time. Not again, never again…

"You can't help him!" Marty shouted in desperation but Kyle ignored him. Steve had returned, and needed him. The man was still a prisoner of his guilt, after all these years. All these long and terrible years.

"Help yourself, before it's too late!"

Too late? But it was too late for Steve. And maybe for himself as well…

Kyle stumbled forward, feeling a tremendous rush of polarizing emotions—guilt, sorrow, frustration, compassion. His heart and mind were flooded by the power of these feelings, and he clung to Steve's forsaken image, unwilling to let him go. It really was too late for him…

A huge figure appeared within the shadows of the forest. Kyle knew immediately that it wasn't Steve, but the one who wielded the horn. Astride a horse blacker than the night itself, with eyes the hue of cinders, a large man—impossibly large—stared outwards at him.

They locked gazes for one brief moment, and then the rider left.

Kyle caught a glimpse as the horseman stormed off into the trees, vanishing completely. But he'd seen enough to utterly terrify him—a long whip held fast within gloved hands, slithering as if alive, steam coming off its coiled length. A quiver of arrows strapped to his back, the notches glittering like emeralds. And worst of all, the antlered rack resting upon his shoulders and neck where a man's *head* should have been.

The horn sounded once more, and Kyle felt a powerful sense of relief, as if a terrible burden had been lifted from his heart, the guilt completely purged away. It was the most wonderful and incredible sensation he'd ever felt in his whole life.

Gone...

But in that same breath, an overwhelming compulsion struck him, at once both terrible and alluring. A wanderlust to see things never before dreamed about, well beyond the scope of man's limited vision, lands unknown to men, traveled only by a few. A dreadful craving for everything wild and dangerous. Unfettered freedom, a release from the confining chains of his life and past.

He swept off into the forest like a shadow shrinking from light, unable to deny the call. Kyle had been remade again—into something else—the burden of guilt purged from his heart and soul.

And now there was a price to be paid...

RETRIBUTION

Walking to the stables, I drank deeply of the crisp spring air, relishing in the vitality of a land flourishing in the midst of a new growing season. Lemon colored dandelions carpeted the pastures, while blue forget-me-nots filled in the gaps of greenery, their delicate petals adding flavor to the wash of more subtle wild flowers that speckled the ground.

What an extraordinary day for a countryside frolic, I thought, waving to Dobson, one of my stable-hands, his cat lean frame scrubbing vigorously at the watering trough. Walking into the cedar framed structure, I went towards the pen of Hickory, my favorite steed, appropriately named for his rich coat. Nickering to me in greeting, I gently rubbed his nose, opening the latch and leading him out to the brilliant noon sunshine. Adjusting my gear, I readied to mount him and checked the stopper to my drinking flask, making sure the precious vintage inside would be secure. I didn't want to be without the Concord grape wine, a familiar companion on my daily skirmishes as I rode the boundaries of my property.

Pausing as I sat atop the horse, I looked over at the ancient stone manor of Grasilt, home to myself and several generations before me. It was not the first time I felt grateful for the placing of my birthright, enabling me to live such a carefree existence. The grounds were impeccable, the hedges trimmed into smooth curves, the ivy kept quietly at bay along the lower walls, and the vegetable garden plowed and lined in rows of perfect order.

I spent many hours digging and planting the host of specimens which helped fill my dinner tables, welcoming the exercise. On the morrow, I thought, would I tackle a new section, since the nights of lingering frost were long past, after an uncommonly brisk winter. Giving a gentle pull on the reins, I turned Hickory and off we went, galloping away beneath the cheerful azure sky overhead and the sprawling meadows.

The turf was firm but pliable beneath the horse's swift and sure feet. Uplifted I was, invigorated by the wind in my face and the hills laying before us. We raced onward, passing fields of billowing grass smelling earthy and peaceful, the powerful animal churning his great legs at a moderate pace. At times I would entertain some of my neighboring friends and we would ride together, speaking of local politics and mutual pleasantries. Even though I was always one to enjoy lighthearted chatter, I must admit that trekking off alone was still my favored choice.

Before us lay a tumbling brook of pristine water, bubbling content-edly across a limestone basin. I halted for a moment, drinking alongside the panting beast and splashing the cool liquid over my face. I felt a bit more adventuresome than usual, and looked upon the forested sides of Grim Man's Hill, looming in the distance and ringed with curling mist, lazily rising upwards from the scattered bogs at its feet.

Even from such a stretch, the region marking the far corners of my lands gave me a twinge of anxiety—a subtle carry-over of hushed warn-ings from the servants. More especially I could remember the grave tone of my deceased Uncle Graystock, as he would sit on the cherry wood high seat before the hearth on bitter wintry nights, reciting the ancient legends and old wive's tales surrounding the mysterious wilder-land. Twice he took me to the fringe of the brooding hillside, pointing out the lack of game and normal sounds of the woodland creatures. He had been of the opinion that a band of wolves prowled the area, thus giving rise to the whispered folklore.

Out of common sense and respect for the stories, I rarely went too close to the hill, but I felt rather peculiar that day, wishing to explore heretofore newer and more challenging territory. Being yet in my early twenties, I still maintained a pinch of adolescent curiosity, and looking back with hindsight, foolishness. A most bothersome thought prodded my mind, leeching on to me like an unwelcome relative, and that was the request in my uncle's will, that I should not venture to Grim Man's Hill. Call it the brilliance of the sun, or folly of youth, it matters not, because I leaped onto Hickory and headed straight towards the forbidden hinterland.

The ride was pleasant for a while as we passed through several fields of mild overgrowth, nothing to thwart the progress of my able steed. I gave him periodic treats, unwilling to push his limits. There were days when I gave him his head, and he would plummet forward at a breath-taking gait, but I was quite content to journey with relaxed ambition.

I chided myself, even laughing, thinking to save Hickory's strength in the chance we were pursued by marauding wolves. Nonsense, I sneered. Maybe there was a bit of historical fact rooted in truth about the hill, but certainly not to the extent of endangerment by untamed beasts.

The ground began to slope downward as we entered into lowlands marked by numerous watercourses and soggy tufts of weed. I slowed our pace to avoid the deeper mud, and wiped the perspiration off my forehead, which had become lightly damp from the humidity.

Bullfrogs croaked ominously further ahead, deep-throated dwellers of the dank fen. Cattails and pickerel weed lined the shallow pools which dotted the region, shadowed by the mossy trunks of vast hoary trees that waged silent battles overhead, grasping with crooked fingers for the warmth of an elusive sun, a stranger to the shrouded swamp. Lichen hung from the peeling bark like the beards of wizened men, hunched over in poses of unhurried contemplation.

Although I had traveled little more than an hour from my estate, I was entering a foreign land, home to crafty scavengers and moisture-loving vegetation. I felt uninvited, and reconsidered my intentions.

No, I would not turn back, I thought, unstoppering my flask and smacking my lips at the fruity beverage. The liquid warmed my veins and soothed the heaviness in my heart, and I pushed onward. I pulled out a fat, round apple from my pouch, biting deeply and savoring the sweet-ness, calming the tomcat-rumbling of my stomach and at the same time banishing the imps of my imagination. Feeding the core to Hickory, I lessened the pace and noticed the increasing density of the forest.

The earth was growing firmer as we approached the foot of Grim Man's Hill. I wondered how it would look from the top of the bluff, and if the trees were thinner. As I gazed around at the persistent mist, my conclusion was that the entire hill was enveloped in perpetual gloom, and no view could be seen from even the higher reaches.

It certainly made for an interesting place, and it was not difficult to understand the hesitation the locals felt about the area. The dreary atmosphere, isolation, and the occasional howling of wolves at hunt (I heard none myself so far)—all would succeed in lending substance to the darker musings of a countryman's mind, I thought. While thinking such notions, a movement to my left broke the pensive moment, and I halted the horse, gazing intently at a cluster of brambles.

There it was again, a slight shifting in the brush, and I waited for the creature to reveal itself.

A masked face peered out from the cover, and I grinned at the sight of a sizable raccoon, foraging along the ground for food. My amusement turned into mild surprise, for I knew the animal was a nocturnal hunter. True, it was dark under the eaves of the forest, but not to the extent of being comparable to night. The raccoon might be sickened, and I decided to veer away, urging the horse onward.

After several minutes, the incident was forgotten, and I took in the trappings of this strange region, aware of the deepening silence and lack of larger game. Beyond the swamp roamed great herds of deer, and I had observed at least a dozen earlier in the day, but not here. The air felt warm and oppressive under the canopy of gnarled branches, and I unbuttoned my jacket, tasting salty beads of sweat on my upper lip. The horse grew increasingly restless, but I continued forward, hoping to gain the higher elevations of the hill before mid-afternoon.

Scattered about the ground were boulders of varying shapes and sizes, along with jagged crests of rock bulging from the earth, signifying our encroachment to the central region of the hill. In front of us appeared a cracked stump, and perched on top was an opossum, the creature's nose sniffing at us in curiosity.

I frowned at the presence of yet another animal which normally awakened only at night to search for its food. The creature quickly scampered away, looking very well-fed and acting precisely to character. A rabid beast would behave unpredictably, lacking in fear and consistency—this opossum was neither. Recalling my own memory of such encounters, I could only recollect ever seeing one or two such creatures visible during the daytime, and this over an expanse of my life.

Odd. Very odd.

What a peculiar land, I thought. Why did the woodland creatures break from deeply-rooted instincts and change their eating habits? What was the reason?

I had no answer, and shrugged away such speculation as a gray wall loomed before us. A fairly steep cliff of unknown proportions blocked the path, and I pressed the horse to the right, attempting to find an easier route. On foot, I could have scaled the crag, but that would mean tying the horse and ascending in uncertainty, finding a way through the gloom and risking separation from my steed, a most uncomfortable possibility in Grim Man's Hill.

We stomped onward for a good ten minutes, and I craned my neck up, wondering as to the height of the precipice and what could be found there. Apprehensive I felt, but at the same time unsatiated, guessing at the mysterious summit of the hill.

As we circled the peak, I could locate no passage that would enable the horse to accompany me. Adding to this was a pessimism for climbing to the top, chancing misdirection or injury. Sighing to myself, I halted the horse for a moment, taking a draught of wine. My thirst saved both our skins, for a tremendous rumbling rang out from above, followed by a cracking that sounded like a peal of thunder.

An enormous tree fell from a gap in the cliff, maybe thirty or more yards overhead, crashing against the rocks and landing dangerously close to us. The horse nickered in fright, tossing me backwards and roughly to the dirt. Rolling with the fall, I fell upon my right leg, wincing in pain as it buckled under me.

My head must have struck a rock and everything went dark.

«««—»»»

I awakened to a wretched aching in my leg and a steady throbbing in the back of my head. At first my vision was blurry, but I regained my senses and remembered the freak event. Assuredly my ankle was sprained, and I pushed off the ground, examining myself for further injury, finding none. I was fortunate. But where was the horse?

There was no sign of the beast anywhere, and I whistled loudly, a signal to call attention. Cursing under my breath, I stared at the carnage before me. The fallen tree was immense, the twisted roots wider in girth than my abdomen. A few more yards and I would have been crushed beneath the massive wood. I moved forward, trying to determine the species, but the bark was so old and rotten as to be unrecognizable. Even spreading my arms wide, I would have failed miserably to encompass the breadth of the tree.

Shaking my head in amazement, I noticed an unusual scent coming from somewhere, a sweet smell but very unlike the sap or mustiness I might have expected. Sharp and extraordinary was the aroma, and I walked closer to the trunk. The wood was rent asunder, revealing a rotted cavity inside, directly beneath a circular bole. From here came the queer fragrance, and I peered into the exposed interior, gasping in surprise.

An utterly grotesque sack lay within—a membranous, crimson-tinged pouch measuring several feet in circumference. Steaming fluid seeped from the ghastly tissue, and it looked like the under wing of a bat, lacking any fur. I was overwhelmed with revulsion, and gagged at the source of the powerful aroma. Never had I set eyes on something as horrendous as what now lay before me.

Was it an egg sack, I thought? But of what? I had seen large clusters of spider nests, and they were repugnant, filled with hordes of tiny spiderlings, but the object before me was much bigger, though, and I was baffled. My heart stopped then as I saw movement from within the sack. Something was struggling to break free...

I stepped back a pace, watching in dreadful fascination as a slimed talon burst through the layer of membrane, a limb of four digits ending in wicked claws. The tear widened as more of the monstrous creature pressed outward, covered in coats of the hideous mucus-like substance, and I was frozen in shock.

My head felt giddy and I nearly swooned as the creature continued to rip apart the confining sack. When I saw its face, I knew that it had to be killed.

A pair of yellow eyelids sat atop a small, greenish head ringed with horned ridges, a slitted mouth gaping like a fish out of water, with cruel, marrow-white fangs protruding from the orifice and eating the membrane. My stomach churned with loathing, and I nearly jumped out of my skin at the sound of something huffing behind me.

It was Hickory, stamping a hoofed foot and looking extremely agitated. I rejoiced at seeing the return of my mount, and fixed my attention once again on the unbelievable creature emerging from the tree. Moving swiftly, I reached for a thick branch and brought the wood down with all my strength onto the skull of the nightmare before me.

I connected solidly, and felt a disgusting crunch of bone through the stick. Unwilling to give the thing a chance to escape, I rained several more blows on its head, and the creature shrieked pathetically, crying out two more times before laying still. Shuddering in horror, I lowered the branch and felt my flesh grow numb as a blood-curdling wail echoed from somewhere far off in the shrouded heights above—a scream of utter despair and agony which could not possibly belong to any creature I had ever known.

No, I thought. This can't be real.

Several times the shriek fell upon my disbelieving ears, and I staggered back towards my horse, tripping over broken boughs and falling rudely to the ground. Frantic, I managed to crawl across the soil, shaking like a feverish man, and reached the horse, grabbing the reins and trying to mount.

After a number of fruitless attempts, I failed to gain the saddle, but fear drove my efforts and then I was up, turning Hickory's head and going back along the cliff, angling away from the hill. I was drenched in a cold sweat, trying to rationalize my situation as we plodded forward.

I was unsuccessful. My mind swam in a sea of confusion and dread.

Holding on desperately to the reins, I felt the alarm in the horse's erratic gait, knowing that the animal sensed, or possibly smelled, the unseen predator. My imagination tormented me with visions of a larger version of the creature I had struck down. Long, deadly claws, a mouth lined with razor-sharp teeth, a head crested with bony spikes. These features alone were enough to drive me insane with fright, but another, even more horrible fact reared itself beyond even these attributes.

On the back of the infant creature had rested a pair of folded wings.

I glanced skyward, terrified of what might descend upon me from the darkness above. My knuckles whitened from the fierce grip I kept on the cords. I dared not think of being alone and horseless in that forsaken place.

The minutes rolled by, time meaningless, my only thought to reach familiar and friendly lands once again, and put Grim Man's Hill far behind. The day was growing late, and we reached the dismal bog unmolested, welcoming even that lusterless region.

Achromatic seemed the forest, and I voiced silent pleas to escape the terrible denizen of the highlands, the unspeakable creature that lurked among the sheltered heights. I knew the consequence of my act immediately after hearing that appalling scream of agony—I had destroyed the offspring of some monstrous, nightmarish beast, existing only in the whispered ramblings of superstitious common folk.

The truth slapped across my face like a physical blow. Would that I had respected the warnings, and strayed not from well-traveled paths. My hope was that the creature would not leave the boundaries of its territory, but stay deep within the forest.

As we emerged from the swamp, I breathed a bit easier, but still glanced overhead. The further we went, the more impossible the event seemed to appear. Long shadows covered the woods, and evening was nigh, finding us miles from the estate. I could not relax for an instant, and constantly looked behind my shoulder, fearing the worst. When at last the trees broke open, I set the horse loose, and we raced across the quiescent fields in a thundering of kicked dirt, leaving small clouds of dust in our wake.

It was like glimpsing the treasure at the base of a rainbow as the manor appeared on the horizon, the family pennant waving in the breeze, noble and patient. The walls of the estate greeted me with adamant confidence, and I felt courage rising up from the depths of my blackest horror. To only be secure within the house, surrounded by my servants—then I could dispel the tide of madness, entrench my fortitude, and take measures to defend against the creature.

Torches were already lighted against the coming of nightfall, and pride welled inside my chest at the fixtures of order which overlapped the estate.

Discipline, loyalty.

Twelve servants were housed within the manor, all at my beck and call, and I felt genuine affection, even considering them as family, since I had no living relatives remaining. I tied the horse to a wooden rail outside the entrance, and limped up the flagstone path towards the main doorway. The metal entry was closed, and I pushed it forward, listening to the creaking hinges.

A small chamber lay within, containing passages to either side, but I ignored them, going straight ahead and into the inner courtyard, where I would find several of my men busy with evening chores.

I walked beneath the carved archway, molded into the shape of a resting lion, and stepped onto the smooth, cobblestone path. The area was wide, crossing several dozen yards, bordered on every side by granite walls. There I paused, staring at the balcony of the master chamber, searching for a sign of movement, but not from any servants. I gazed upward with stale eyes, looking for the presence of my monstrous adversary.

Then I felt my chest constrict in a vice of pure terror...

The servants were there already, motionless on the alcove. Carefully placed so that I would see their unmoving forms immediately, strewn over the metal railing like puppets—the creature had arrived before I did.

Whimpering, trembling with shaking limbs, I waited for the end. I gazed up at the cloudless sky, the full, bloated moon, which seemed to be leering down at me, holding dark secrets within its celestial body. Several long moments I waited there, too afraid to move.

The horror eventually broke inside me at some point—I don't know if I stood there for seconds or minutes, but my fear molded into action and I sprinted to the courtyard door. My boots clicked loudly upon the stone, and I knew the creature would be alerted to my presence if it hovered nearby.

As I ran, I sensed more than saw a large shadow above me, an unspeakable silhouette of something which could only exist in nightmares. My entire body felt as if it were encased within ice, fear threatening to overwhelm and strike me to the stone. The door lay a few yards before me, but every step dragged on. Too slow, I thought.

If I could but gain the opening, maybe I could yet escape the beast. Charging forward, I grabbed the handle and turned, as a quiet *swoosh* descended upon me. I heard the low huffing of the creature's breath, a foul odor gagging me of rot and dead things. I felt something cold upon my back, but didn't know if it were the spider-chills of fear or the talons of the creature.

I continued turning the handle, and my alarm grew to a terrible new level as I realized the door was locked—I was trapped, fully exposed to the monster's wrath. I covered my head to ward off the coming blows, and dove to the ground, hoping to elude the creature and flee to another doorway. Rolling along the stone, the expected slash of angry claws didn't find me, and I chanced a look to see where it had flown to, and then I spotted it...

Perched on the upper turret like a hideous gargoyle, the creature was motionless, the wings resting on its scaled back. The eyes watched me from above—wicked yellow pinpricks, intelligent and unblinking. I returned the gaze for several seconds, gauging the distance between myself and a side door which I had missed seeing earlier, as it was partly open.

The beast measured me—that I could tell. Whether in caution, or otherwise, I didn't know or care, and I darted away, reaching the door quickly and slamming it shut behind me. I slunk to the ground, worming my way to the lowest reaches of the keep and cringing from every imagined sound or vague shadow, barring the great oaken doors shut and finally collapsing to the cold floor. I slept like the undead that evening, my nightmares reliving the horrific events as the creature stalked me to the end.

«««—»»»

And that is the greatest, most puzzling thing of all, for the end did not arrive that night. Or for several more following nights.

Was it satisfied, thinking that it succeeded in slaying what it considered to be *my* offspring, the servants? Had its blood thirst been quenched? It had chased me down to my own courtyard, held my fate within its grisly talons, and let me live.

I do not know the reason...

Within the lowest reaches of the wine cellars I hide, bolting the doors and jumping at every noise. It has been many days, but I will not venture forth, and expose myself to the angry skies above, and what may lurk there.

The answer eludes me. Has the creature released its hatred? Returned to Grim Man's Hill for good? Or does it merely bide time, tormenting me with the dream of escape, taunting me to make a bid for freedom.

I think I understand its motives.

Perhaps it has a more sinister scheme, playing a deadly cat's paw game, making me suffer in silent, constant terror, until I go mad and take a chance at leaving the manor.

In my mind's eye I can see its abominable form, circling the pinnacles and walls of my home, which has been transformed into the most terrible of prisons. It patiently watches, and waits, for me to run like a frightened rabbit, before rendering one final, dreadful act.

Of retribution.

IN THE NIGHT, HEELS CLICKING

"**A**lways the skeptic."

Kathy looked up at David over the rim of her mug. His gray eyes sparkled with humor, and a hint of something else. She could never tell if it was sarcasm or good nature. They sat at her favorite table in the coffee shop, nestled in the far corner, where the lights were dim and a small nook gave them a degree of privacy. The aroma was pleasant, a mixture of fresh roasted blends, warm and soothing.

"My opinions are practical, scientific, and well-researched. As you already know. I keep an open mind, but when it comes to the supernatural, there is no evidence to support your beliefs." Kathy waved a hand for emphasis, waiting for his rebuttal. She always found this man to be so intriguing, in several ways. Darkly handsome, he was dressed in impeccable black, now wearing a long coat with matching scarf. His shoes were polished obsidian, a pair of leather gloves placed neatly on the table. A short, pointed beard edged the bottom of his chin, and a trimmed mustache complimented the 'scoundrel' look, which she had labeled him soon after their first meeting.

In reply to her statement, David merely chuckled, which succeeded in annoying Kathy even more. Annoyed, not angered…

"Ah, the boring vision of the pragmatic scientist, who puts everything beneath her microscope, and always manages to extract an explanation which satisfies her mundane logic. Such a sad way of looking at things."

Raising an eyebrow, Kathy replied. "And you, who romanticizes everything, finding a ghost in every shadow, an angel within every cloud, and a question long after the answer is given." She drained the rest of her drink.

David failed to relent. "But don't you at least *wish* there was something more?" He leaned back in his chair, his confidence evident. He possessed an incredible ability to hide uncertainty from her—or any other weakness—for that matter. And this only made him a more fascinating figure. Kathy had never met someone who evoked such strong emotions in her, both frustration and attraction. Their friendship was casual, but she had the unnerving feeling that she played right into his hands, for whatever reason. She secretly hoped he would ask her out on a formal date, but so far he hadn't even come close. And she made a point *not* to be the one asking him out. Somehow, she thought he knew this, and played the game all the more cleverly. Damn…

"No, sorry to disappoint you, David. I stopped believing in fairies when I was a child. Never had an invisible friend, no spirits haunted my house. I've never seen a flying saucer either. But I do find the gullibility of others to be rather amazing. And *that's* why I'm so good at my job." She allowed herself a smug little smirk of her own, daring him to denounce her success as editor of *Slapping Reality,* a respected quarterly journal which emphasized cutting edge science, with a keen eye on debunking folklore and assumptions, both new and old.

"I think you're priceless, my dear. A gem."

His reply left her feeling down another point in the game…Somehow, he always maneuvered around her direction, never showed anything but cheerfulness and that nagging hubris, further aggravating her by what he *didn't* say…

"Maybe I'll give you a slot in an upcoming issue. How would you like that? You're a tough nut to crack. Of course, like many others, without a shred of evidence you'll only be piping out an empty philosophical thesis, although I'm sure it will be written superbly."

David laughed quietly, a smile covering his face but his eyes remained shrouded.

Kathy shrugged, then shook her head, the medium-length red hair brushing her shoulders. "Every artist I've ever met was a bit eccentric. You're no exception, I guess."

"I'm working on a painting just for you." His smile intact, he stared amusingly at her. This took her by surprise.

"Really? And what does it look like? I'm flattered."

She *was.*

"It's not finished—yet. Soon, perhaps."

"No hints? Come on, you have me wondering now. I hope it's nothing perverted."

"I love your sense of humor, Kathy. Really. But your question is *my* perception of yourself. This is what I see, and know." He paused, but she was silent, waiting to hear more. Then he continued. "Inside, I see a woman who yearns for release, to embrace the universe and all its wonders. And that's the *only* hint I'll give you."

She frowned. "An interpretation of my inner self? You think you know me so well? Don't be too sure of yourself. You'll be sadly disappointed."

He only shook his head in response.

"What's the background at least? This coffee shop?" She grinned.

"Not quite. Still working on the setting. Shadings of light and dark. And gray. The stage of humanity in three simple tones. Faith and disbelief. Choice."

Kathy cleared her throat. "With me in the middle of all this, I suspect?"

David folded his arms together, his gaze never leaving her green eyes.

"Well. Keep your secrets to yourself for now. I'm flattered that I pose such inspiration for your artwork. But, I'm going home. They're calling for snow this evening, the first of the year. And I need to proof an article before I call it a night."

He rubbed a smooth hand against the table's edge. "It's coming. I can taste it in the air, feel it on my skin. The cold reaches out to you. It's easy to understand the elements, once you're attuned to them. All you need to do is open your heart."

"Metaphors and whimsical musings." Kathy sighed, standing. "You really should take up poetry. Now that's a promising talent I see in you, David. Although I'm sure your artwork is quite impressive as well."

"I am what I am." His hand grazed his chest. "Sweet dreams, my dear girl. I'll see you here Wednesday, right?"

"Always. Unless I'm snatched away by spooks or worse. Good night."

"Good night to you. And pleasant dreams," he replied.

She could still hear him laughing quietly to himself when she walked away. How aggravating he could be! And one of these days, she hoped he would actually offer to walk her home.

One of these days…

Kathy passed through the business district on her way back home. The coffee shop was only a few blocks from her apartment, and the area was pleasant and safe, with people always traveling between the various stores, bars, or restaurants. And besides, she never stayed out very late, leaving usually by nine. The street lamps cast a strong glow, lighting the night, and she shivered as cool hands prodded at her, the wind looking for purchase in the openings of her winter coat. It *did* feel like snow tonight.

She walked by the old church, glancing up the cobblestone pavement leading to its front entrance. A marvelous piece of local history, it was a replica of a famous European Gothic cathedral, although she couldn't place the name. Electric candles peered out at her from the stained-glass windows, and the row of saplings which skirted the main walkway quivered against the breeze. Now leafless, they appeared skeletal, the branches poking out at odd angles.

Siding the structure was a narrow alley, and sometimes she walked through it, avoiding the extra two blocks. She felt cold, and decided to go that way. She turned, heading towards the church entrance. Normally the basement was lighted, as members stayed late, either in preparation for an upcoming bazaar, or rehearsing for choir practice. Tonight, the building seemed empty and quiet. It didn't bother her though, as she felt very comfortable so close to home. She even was on friendly terms with the pastor, and would exchange pleasant conversation with him when they happened on a chance meeting.

Kathy avoided the front steps and pivoted to the side instead, where an opening loomed before her, a tunnel of about fifty yards leading to the opposite street where she lived. Although the corridor appeared shadowed, there was enough light cast from the opposing street lamps to reveal anyone who might be inside. And it was clearly unoccupied as she entered.

She walked through, unhurriedly, and was nearing the middle of the tunnel when she heard a strange noise. Pausing, she peered ahead, trying to discover the source. There was nothing to be seen, and she looked over her shoulder, a bit fearful, wondering if someone was entering behind her. But the front of the church had been empty, and there really was no place for someone to remain hidden. Perhaps a parishioner had left the church right after she'd entered the corridor.

But no, there wasn't any sign of someone following.

Biting her lip, she continued several yards, and then heard the sound again. She angled her head, listening. To her surprise, it came from overhead somewhere, in the unseen heights above. To her left was an old apartment building, now vacant, the windows staring dark and silent from the brick and stone. Echoes drifted down, a sharp clicking, as of heels smacking against the hard surface.

Was someone working on the roof? The apartment was for sale, so anything was possible. She mentally shrugged, then continued walking, reaching the end and plunging into the full light. People shuffled along the sidewalk, some talking, others laughing. Putting aside the odd noise, Kathy made for her apartment, shortly entering and retiring early.

The taste of coffee was strong in her mouth, and the arms of sleep soon claimed Kathy, teasing her with images of David and his confident smile.

«««—»»»

It was Wednesday evening, and Kathy was sitting at her usual table in the coffee shop, a frown wrinkling her face, more of a pout than anything else. She folded a pad of notebook paper next to her mug, having just read the contents. It was a short message from David, given to her by Marcie, the counter girl. He was unable to make it that night. His agent had booked a last-minute appointment with a visiting dealer, and he would be away most of the evening. Kathy knew she was childish for being upset—after all, they had no real relationship beyond meeting in the shop itself. It was rather strange, when she cared to give it much thought.

Admittedly, she did.

Maybe *too* much lately. She definitely felt a growing enticement to the dark, mysterious man. And she knew so little of him…He was an artist, and lived in a studio somewhere north of Bagwich Park. Every time she tried to learn more about him, he somehow managed to steer the conversation, focusing on the symbolism of his art, and twisting his current projects into slight philosophical jabs at her insistently logical approach to life and her own work. She bit her lip in frustration, chiding herself for succumbing to this annoying little habit.

Her coffee tasted especially good tonight—it must have been

today's shipment of beans, she mused. She jotted mental notes about the research sitting back on her desk—a series of linked articles on circus attractions and how they had given security and a place of belonging to those suffering from severe medical conditions. People in recent centuries had considered them to be tainted with the supernatural, many times cast from society and victimized. In particular, those stricken with a malady which caused excessive hair growth, who might very well have been the source for lycanthropic legends. No werewolves, only misunderstood ailments. Like all things weird and fantastic, it was a simple matter of having the wrong facts.

She was creating passages in her mind, parts of the text which she would write down later. Unfortunately, whenever a strong statement materialized, a suitably descriptive passage, David's face soon appeared from memory, effectively shattering the creativity of her own inner voice. She knew it was useless tonight. The man was certainly an enigma. And a handsome one at that…

Sighing, Kathy finished her drink and placed a ten dollar bill on the table, standing up to leave. "Good night." She nodded to Marcie who smiled in return. Opening the door, Kathy immediately felt the icy clutch of the wind, and a snowflake glided onto her nose. Stepping onto the sidewalk, she looked up, admiring the glistening white powder falling downwards. The angry gray sky earlier in the day had made good on its promise—a storm was definitely in the beginning stages. She trudged forward, the ground already conceding purchase to the assault from above. Pulling her jacket tighter, she was thankful her apartment was only a short distance away.

Shoppers and others bustled along, and she caught snips of conversation about the weather. It was early December, and the holiday rush was evident in the growing number of late-night pedestrians. Kathy waved to a lady she recognized as a regular at the coffee shop, although she didn't know the woman's name.

So many strangers in the world, she thought to herself. And when do you *really* know someone? Kathy had friends at the office, but only two or three who were fairly close; the rest of her co-workers were merely acquaintances. And that term meant a lot. Close. There was a huge gap between real friendship and everything else…Kathy also realized that seldom would she permit anyone to pass her self-imposed barrier. Which was exactly why David frustrated her so much! She *wanted* to let down her guard, had implied it on several occasions now, and he'd subtly refused her advances. He always seemed in so much control, and she couldn't shake the feeling that he was toying with her. A polite smile, well-placed remark, and the conversation would be casually diverted. On his terms.

Frowning, she almost passed the church without knowing it. She quickly turned, nearly slipping. Holding back a curse, Kathy went towards the tunnel, looking forward to the warmth of her apartment…and a hot bath tonight. Now *that* would be good therapy for her social failings, she decided.

The church was dark, and Kathy entered the passage, peering ahead, but it was dim tonight, the snow obscuring vision. She'd only gone several yards when a noise echoed from somewhere above, and she stopped. Remembering the other night, she listened with curiosity, gazing skyward. She heard the sound again, a sharp clicking, then a tapping. Men working tonight, in this weather? The notion seemed ridiculous. Glancing behind her, and then in front, she appeared to be alone. Actually, she only recalled seeing one or two people in here before, and one had been the pastor.

Kathy nibbled on her lip, and then pressed onward. It was too cold outside to worry about the strange evening activities of contractors…

Taking short but quick steps, she hurried towards the end, where it gradually became a bit lighter from the street lamps. Then the noise drifted downwards once more, faster and louder this time. Angling her neck, she spotted something moving, near the top, along the side of the building. It appeared to be sticking out from the wall, steadily advancing higher. Her mouth opened in amazement.

Something was moving up the wall…

Quickly as the bizarre vision appeared, the thing reached the top and vanished from sight. She was stunned. It had looked like a figure of some kind, standing upright, but running impossibly along the side of the building. There was no way, she thought… Absolutely *no* way that it was a person. And during that brief glimpse, the noise had accompanied the movement, like boots—heels, clicking away as it ascended. A small circle of light had also flashed, right when it disappeared. A speck of bluish light.

Kathy was too confused to act for a few moments. Then the cold pressed in on her, and she wondered if the whole thing had been only her imagination, from the snow and gloom. Regardless, she quickened her pace and passed through the end of the tunnel, anxious for her own warm apartment. Everything was normal on the street, and the sights and sounds of a thriving community welcomed her.

But had she really seen something in the alley?

An uneasiness stayed with her that night, up until she finally fell asleep, her bedroom curtains thrown wide so she could admire the snowfall which painted the streets in a coat of shimmering white.

And sometime during the night her dreams were disturbed by a slight *tapping* sound, but when consciousness fought to shrug off the night-wings of slumber, the noise ended and her fantasies turned pleasant.

«««——»»»

It was Friday night, and Kathy sat in the coffee shop, staring curiously at David's humorous face. He wagged a finger at her, the long nails tapping the rim of his mug. "My dear girl, you're working a bit too hard. Did you ever consider the implications of your position?"

Although he had successfully diverted a previous question, Kathy failed to hide the smile on her beaming face. Seeing David tonight had lightened her mood considerably. "Of course, I have no idea what you're talking about...You know, I think you're a modern day Renaissance Man. All romance and style. It's a wonder you're still single." A not-so-subtle hint, she knew.

He folded lean hands together. "My trade demands my constant attention. It's a lifestyle not easily understood. Now, back to my question. You may not realize this, but the process of constant debunking—and that is a rather awkward word—creates a layer of negativity, a barrier of the mind against embracing possibility."

"Possibility? Of what?" Kathy shook her head in confusion. David and his philosophical statements...

Now David sat back in his chair, absently toying with his shirt collar. "Of everything. Anything. Don't you *see*?" His smirk was absolutely devilish.

"No, I *don't*," she admitted. "Really, I don't." Shrugging her shoulders, she tossed her hair to the right, an almost unconscious attempt at open flirtation.

"I would think a girl born and raised in the bosom of London itself, surrounded by all the unique trappings, with such majestic history and colorful hauntings, *might* have just a degree more of open-mindedness."

"Am I disappointing you?" She regretted the statement instantly.

There was a slight pause, but then David leaned forward. "Not in the least. Faith wears many masks. Some blatant, others darker. I'm a patient man."

I'm an impatient girl, though.

"Going back to my point…" He paused for emphasis, waiting until she screwed her face up and frowned. "Your *disbelief* is a result of something much deeper, and more profound. I think you've encountered something quite extraordinary, perhaps in your childhood, and have tried to bury it. Thus your career and steadfastness…Living proof, dear girl. You're actually looking for answers to something you can't explain. Smoke and mirrors, all the rest. In the end, you don't believe in your own work."

It was a powerful statement, and Kathy fought against a quick retort. Was he baiting her? To what purpose? Why should her work evoke such strong words from him? He didn't come off so much as being rude, condescending, but more like a teacher to a well-loved if wayward student. David's notion struck a chord inside her, and she felt extremely uneasy. Strange things *had* happened in her childhood, but how would he know anything about her past? And nothing had ever convinced her that her belief system was flawed. Imagination and suggestion were companions to childhood and the night. Well-known companions. Not spooks…

"Sorry, but you're way off on this one, my *dear*." Kathy stood, reaching into her purse. Attraction or not, she didn't feel like explaining herself to this intriguing man anymore—at least not tonight. She suddenly felt tired. It *had* been a long day at work.

"Leaving already? I hope I didn't upset you." His face appeared genuinely concerned, but his eyes glittered with an inner fire. Like suppressed laughter. Was she really being played this badly?

"Not at all. But you're wrong, and that's all there is to it. I have a long day tomorrow, weekend deadlines. Next week maybe?"

David stood, his tall form meshing with the shadows in the corner. "Certainly. And I'll get the tab, the least I can do." That devilish smile again…"Take care, Kathy. We'll continue our discussion. Don't be too harsh to judge me—I have this nasty habit of trying to bring people in touch with their hidden emotions. It's harmless, you must understand. Art. I approach life as one interwoven project, waiting to be tweaked. And maybe that's why I remain alone…" His words drifted off, his tone edged with sadness, and Kathy found it impossible to tell if this was an invitation or a rebuttal.

"Well, good night, David. Thanks for paying. But listen, we're all guilty of trying to rationalize everyone else, you know?" She turned, flashing him a quick smile. Kathy walked away, and she could have sworn he laughed quietly behind her.

«««—»»»

The streets around her were more subdued this night.

A fresh coat of snow had fallen earlier in the afternoon, accumulating several inches. This and a biting northeasterly wind had succeeded in keeping the normal parade of shoppers at home, blanketed within warmer comforts. Kathy enjoyed her evening activities, however, and had been eager to see her strange friend, especially since he'd been absent on Monday. She'd asked him how his meeting had gone, but the answer given was vague, almost an afterthought. Everything about David reinforced his elusive aura, but this only added to his overall appeal. How completely frustrating, she thought to herself.

There were few cars on the road, and the pavement was slick with ice. She tred carefully, not wanting to slip. As she approached the church, she was surprised to see the downstairs brimming with illumination. There must be some preparation for an upcoming service or other event going on, she mused. The front door opened a crack, and she caught a glimpse of someone poking their head outside. Just as quickly the panel closed.

Kathy had attended a few services there, and always felt a degree of comfort when near its high walls. She made her way towards the alley, her heart catching as she felt her boots skid for a moment. Stepping ahead, she entered, staring at the flakes as they appeared to be growing larger. The storm must be worsening…

Kathy was near the mid-point when she happened to look up. Someone was standing at the other end, near the entrance to her own street.

Obscured by shadows, the stranger was silent and unmoving.

Kathy stopped, feeling a chill snaking along her spine.

If the person had been moving along normally, making their way through the tunnel, she would have been much less suspicious. People were always within hearing range of the short corridor, and she'd always felt safe. Now, she was uncertain.

So she waited there, trying to make out details of the stranger.

Without warning, the figure sprang forward, directly towards her. She didn't have time to react or even think. With amazing speed, the stranger had closed half the distance already.

In a single leap!

Truly frightened, Kathy gasped. To her greater surprise, the person—who looked to be a man cloaked in some type of long coat—veered away from her at the last minute, instead jumping against the side of the vacant building.

Bewildered by the stranger's irrational behavior, she was shocked as the man continued accelerating, now actually running along the wall, *but going upwards...*

She held her breath in fear as the man moved higher, impossibly scaling the wall like it was an ordinary, level pavement. As he raced along, he would jump between fire escapes in his ascent, bobbing and weaving about as if gravity meant nothing. A loud *clicking* accompanied his movements, and quickly he reached the roof, pausing to glare down at her. Pinpricks of blue fire matched her own terrified stare, and hellish laughter drifted downwards.

It was too much for Kathy and she bolted through the tunnel, ignoring the slickness at her feet. She reached the end of the corridor and burst into the street with its welcome lighting. A handful of people trudged along the sidewalk on the other side, oblivious to what she'd seen. No one paid her the slightest attention, all of them eager to reach their own destinations. Kathy stumbled forward, angling straight across the road, not stopping until she made it to the end of the block in front of her own apartment. Fumbling with the key, her breathing was heavy, her heart pounding madly.

She swallowed several times, then hurried up the steps, making certain to lock the door behind her. Shortly she was in her own room, collapsing on the softness of her bed.

What had she seen? Clearly, something incredible. Unexplainable.

And these two adjectives were unfamiliar to her, so her mind urged calmness. Relax, she told herself. Think…

Kathy stood, going into the bathroom and splashing cold water on her face. Stress, she reasoned? Imagination? It had to be the answer.

No, *needed* to be.

Nothing else would suffice.

Leaning on the sink, she recalled David's words, about suppressing her childhood memories, or something to that effect.

"What's happening? Am I going insane?"

She rubbed a hand against her forehead, wiping away the sweat. Something teased her mind, pressing gently, but persistently, for release. But she would have none of it…

Kathy returned to the bedroom and slumped down on blankets. She looked at her bookshelf, and all the scientific texts. The piles of magazines, everything she'd ever written and published. She then walked towards the window, trying to rationalize the events of the evening. It all seemed so strange, unreal. Staring at her reflection framed against the sheen of snow on the streets, she watched in horror as another face appeared, forming from out of the night itself, with dark, striking features. The window swung open, no hand maneuvering the latch.

Cold air blew inside, eager to find a victim for its wintry passion.

The stranger stood on the window ledge, one hand beckoning to her. She backed away.

Blue eyes held her riveted, and smoke curled from the man's lips, as if an inferno smoldered somewhere deep within…

The words were low, compelling. A scent of sulfur drifted in, and Kathy was mesmerized and horrified by the impossible being who now spoke.

"Embrace the night. I've been waiting for you."

She found herself unable to act, sobbing and frightened, but also enchanted somehow. Diabolically handsome, this enigmatic intruder seemed part shadow, part substantial. Real or imagined?

The stranger moved, and she heard the clicking of sharp heels against the cold stone.

"Take my hand, and we'll leap together, Kathy."

His breath reeked of ashes, and he opened one palm, the skin pale and lifeless.

"Believe in me. You did as a child."

She whimpered, confused and afraid, as old visions heaved themselves up from the black maw of her memory. Noises outside from her childhood home in London. Invisible footsteps. Faint laughter. The night, whispering to her on the wings of fantasy. Long hours huddling beneath her blankets, eyes tightly shut. And worse yet were the rumors spoken by adults, about a strange apparition roaming the streets and rooftops of the city...Heels clicking.

In the background, she heard David's voice, but couldn't locate the source. Was it coming from inside the building, or could it be a deception woven by the stranger? It was impossible to tell.

"Choose wisely."

Kathy hesitated, scant inches away from the window and its diabolical lurker.

"I'll set you free."

Was this what she really wanted? Had her denial been the motivation behind her career? She blinked, but the vision remained. Where should she place her faith? David had captured her heart, but refused her advances. What could this fantastic being offer? Something which had been lacking inside of her?

The stranger waited, and she felt his hot breath on her neck. It was both wicked and sensual at the same time.

"Believe..."

And then she took his hand, and together they leaped into the night.

DEVIL MAN
OF THE HOLLOW

Our expedition reached the top of a craggy hillside which had impeded progress for most of the day. Drenched with sweat, bloodied arms and hands, the trek had not been a pleasant one. The mainly British group consisted of twelve men, including myself and four hired locals to lead us through this relatively unfamiliar region of the jungle. We were skirting the edge of the present frontier, and now walked in areas that none of our race had ever seen before.

We were the first—the toughest breed among men. Explorers of the vast jungle, and heirs to the fortunes that lay in wait beyond the horizon.

"All right. We break among those rocks near the top. Move on."

Exhausted and bruised, the men continued in the direction I had pointed. I was parched with thirst and my stomach groaned for a reprieve, but one learns to ignore such inconveniences if he wishes to survive long in the jungle, and I had been there for the past seven years.

As we gathered around an outcropping of a few boulders, I at once noticed a change in our guides. They had led us through numerous miles of some of the deepest undergrowth we had ever seen without so much as a hint of uncertainty. These natives knew the land and were in communion with its nature. To exist in such a harsh climate demanded respect and understanding—they possessed both. There could be no mistakes. An error in the jungle meant death. You needed to gain that knowledge of survival by watching the ones who had persevered and still continued to do so. But now I sensed a conflict of wills being waged between our guides and my man Robinson, so I walked into their midst.

"Is there some confusion here?"

"There does seem to be a problem, sir," Robinson answered. "The trail forks and goes off in different directions. Look here."

I followed his gaze and saw the fork several dozen yards ahead. It seemed the main path went in a southerly route and the smaller path branched to the left almost due east, which was the general vicinity of our destination.

The path edged about the ridge we had come over, then made its way down the other side into a hollow filled with lush vegetation. The trees did not appear to be impassable by any means, and I needed to make some good time here.

Robinson was peering at the map with disdain, the long mustache on his weathered face drooping with disapproval. He shook his head and spoke to Chatra, who was the guide leader. Chatra was pointing at two of his men and they were staring into the hollow. When I considered this later, the two had been shifting their fingers in very strange fashion, and I overlooked it at the time. Queer, I had thought. If only I had taken heed. The movements had been warding-off gestures to whatever presence they feared in the hollow below.

"Sir, seems these two chaps refuse to go down this path, despite the fact that we will probably save over a day getting to the village. Maybe more from the look of it. You can even see the lip of the next ridge. Can't be more than two days march from here, if that. The hill you see is the left overpass of the trail as it cuts straight through the break." Robinson gave me a hard look of confidence and waited for my agreement.

"Well then, what reason do these fellows give for such reluctance? Head hunters? Never any mention before of such. Not in these here parts. Why won't Chatra keep them in line now?"

Robinson shook his head. "They're not from his village, but a smaller one down south. They'll take the main path or start home."

"What? Did you tell them they would forfeit their pay? What think they of that?"

But Robinson had threatened the two already. "They will not change their minds. They insist on going south, and say that we enter the hollow at great peril." As Robinson spoke, he snatched phrases from Chatra for the translation, a guttural dialogue, one which I only partially understood.

"Sir, it seems that this hollow here is some sort of taboo land for them." He looked at me with a slight scowl, which indicated growing annoyance. Robinson had been with me for a long time and was my right hand man. I trusted his instinct.

"Ah, some superstitious nonsense. These natives create the most horrific stories and scare the wits out of themselves. There is no end to the tales they weave. Tell Chatra to offer an additional day's wage, and let's end this rubbish." Now I was becoming impatient.

Robinson beseeched the leader once again but the two held firm. I looked back and the others were relaxing in the afternoon heat, sitting beneath a small grove of trees. All except for Crane, who had been kneeling on one leg, hand shading eyes, staring down to the valley floor.

Crane was a reserved and soft-spoken fellow. The man never once complained and would lend a hand wherever the need was. Family was well off, and he had more education than the rest of the group. His background made him distinguished from the other men, but once they became acquainted there was a strong friendship that had been formed between them. I turned to see how Robinson had fared and the look on his face gave me the answer.

"Well now, if they are so afraid then let them leave," I said. "But what say our man Chatra? Will he go too?"

"No, sir. He says that the tribes around here believe in strange things. He scoffs at such talk. I believe Chatra has spent enough time with civilized men like us than to be frightened by jungle spirits anymore."

Chatra stood with his arms folded, face impassive as usual. There was not an ounce of humor to be found in the tough native. A natural leader of his people, he made an imposing figure. Tall, broad of chest, rippling muscles—these features created an aspect of granite about the man. Immovable, unemotional. Wishing to quench my thirst, I opened my water flask and drank deeply. I peered over the rim and watched as Crane approached.

"Sir."

"What is it, Crane?" There was an odd look on the man's face. He appeared a bit unwell.

"May I have a word with you?" I walked over to him. "Certainly, man. Are you feeling all right?" Crane pulled at his shirt sleeve nervously. Something was bothering him.

"Well, I don't quite know how to answer that question. Maybe feel is the wrong word." The look on his face was puzzling. "Could be there is some truth in what those two fellows are saying." Crane met my gaze unflinchingly. Here was another that I could rely on. Wasn't one to spook at fairy tales.

"Come now, Crane." I replied. "Surely you're not going to say that there is truth in this tale? Too much heat, maybe? You look a shade pale."

He shook his head. Short blond hair, fair skin, eyes without sun wrinkles. Crane was the youngest of us but had knowledge beyond his twenty-five years. "No, not at all. This hollow has a strange taste to it. I was trying to put my finger on it, but I don't know…"

"What do you think, then? Head hunters? Apes? We can take care of these. Have before. Is this your worry, then?" But my guesses were well off the mark.

"No. I would feel better actually if it were such things. Do you know how the jungle always is so full of activity, vibrant? There is a natural order here, and it pulsates with life. And now, this is hard to put into words, but the hollow seems dead. Yes, we can see the plants and trees, but nothing else. There are no birds or animals to be seen. And further yet, although you may think me odd, I have the feeling that we are being watched. By who or what, I don't know."

As I listened to his words, my gaze searched the hollow. There did seem to be a lack of game, but that would point to a large predator. A pride of lions, maybe. To be sure, we would take extra caution. That could be the rationale behind the reluctance of the two men. Probably some unfortunate natives had fallen prey to the beasts and it did not take much in these parts for a new legend to find root.

Even so, scanning the jungle gave me the peculiar sensation that there was indeed something observing us. I attributed the cause being the anxiety of the others and brushed off the notion at once, deciding that we best move ahead by the quickest means possible, and that meant through the hollow. The last thing we needed was to second guess ourselves after we had come so far.

I clapped the man on the back and told him my plan. He was to continue south with our two reluctant guides and stick to the main trail. Another of our group would accompany him and they would make sure those two earned their pay. That left eight men led by Chatra and myself to cut through the hollow and map out a better path for the next company. It was settled.

Robinson and Chatra conversed with the guides and the other men prepared to move on. "Sir, you won't reconsider?" Crane had a look of concern across his youthful features. "Perhaps we can gather a larger group from the village to better search this hollow."

For a brief second, I hesitated, but then my overconfidence came to light.

"My good fellow, I will see you safely on the other side of this bowl. If there is a lion, we will carry his head up to the village and stake it for all to see. The tables will be set and the meat hot as the rest of us will await your arrival. Stray not from the trail and we will meet before the new moon shines again."

With that we wished all good fortune and once again were on the march.

It had been a good couple of hours later when we had descended into the hollow and reached bottom. The way down was not too difficult, but the path was at times hard to follow. There were a number of fallen trees to climb over, and one needed to be ceaselessly vigilant against the presence of poisonous snakes that made the jungle their home.

In the lead were Chatra and Robinson. These men were born trackers. Next followed Edward and Landers, both seasoned hunters and skilled in the ways of the deep jungle. Landers was tall and thin, with several scars on his face from combat. Quick as a cat he was. Edward was a giant of a man, six and a half feet at least. The sight of him alone in several villages was enough to demand their instant respect as he walked among the natives, towering over them.

After this pair came Jamie and Woods, the two with the shortest amount of experience in the wild but still good men. I followed next and the other guide named Saric followed me. We were in hunting formation, with our middle flanking out furthest. My position in the party enabled me to maximize action against any situation that arose and subsequently react at once.

Evening was drawing nigh and our group made decent time. Nothing untoward had occurred and all thoughts of the unusual were at rest. The air was becoming a bit cooler and this was a welcome change from the oppressive heat. The mood was light and some of the men started singing phrases of an old drinking song. This did not bother me, as long as they stayed alert for potential hazards.

They had been singing for a good while, when I slowly began to feel an uneasiness creep over me. I have always placed trust in my own senses, would that I had done so with someone else's.

I surveyed our formation, everything was satisfactory.

Shifting my gaze skyward, I could make out the dim glimmer of early evening stars as they began to dot the heavens. It was getting late. A suitable campsite would have to be picked shortly, but I was certain our lead men had already started to search for one. The foliage in this area was not too badly overgrown, so they would more than likely call for a halt soon. Nothing out of the ordinary. The men were still singing, but they seemed in good spirits and remained observant.

Then it struck me.

It was the singing that bothered me, for there was no other sound to be heard. Since we had traveled deeper into the hollow, there hadn't been the normal jungle noises one grew accustomed to. Birds, insects, wildlife. Maybe during the descent there had existed some activity, but now there was none.

Was I the only one of us to notice?

I peered over my shoulder to check on Saric. His face confirmed my own disquiet. He gave me a knowing look, and his eyes darted nervously left and right. The native looked back into the jungle we'd left behind, and then he stopped. Immediately I gave a quick whistle, and my men ceased their movement.

With the singing now ended, a deathly quiet fell on the surrounding jungle. There was no other sign of life besides our own to be heard. We were intruders in a hostile land—my apprehension grew.

"Men, hold guard." Robinson made his way back towards me as the group attained a defensive posture. I reached Saric's side and the native crouched down. His hunting knife was clenched in his hand and he looked like a cat ready to spring.

"Sir, what is…" My swift gesture silenced Robinson instantly. I pointed to Saric and he understood my caution. Slowly Robinson crept back to us and went to the native's side. In hushed tones he spoke in the tribal dialect for several moments. They both peered intently into the jungle behind us, and spoke some more. I turned to check on the others but all seemed to be in order. No one had dropped their vigilance.

By now it was almost fully dark, and a slight mist rose sluggishly amongst the undergrowth. It had an eerie effect on our minds, being coupled with the lack of any sounds reaching our ears.

Some of the men started to become restless, and what had been a strong and confident force only minutes ago was now experiencing pangs of self-doubt and trepidation. The atmosphere was laden with tension—it was palpable. Invisible tendrils of fear reached out of the encircling darkness, searching for a foothold to latch onto. A weakened spirit can lead to panic and despair in the great jungle. I had seen it before.

Robinson left Saric's side and approached. He seemed unnerved, and that worried me. "What is it, man?" I asked him. "What does he see?"

"He's not sure what it is, but Saric is convinced we are being followed. Even more so, we are being hunted by something. It is noiseless and out of sight, but there can be no doubt. He does not understand the nature of this creature or its purpose, but it tracks us. Ever since sundown."

His words sent a cold shiver through me. I had known the answer before it had been spoken.

"Did he see it, then? Maybe we can identify the beast, then perhaps ensnare it."

Robinson ran his hand absently over the rifle he shouldered and considered his reply.

"Saric says that he caught a quick glimpse of it. About half an hour back he became aware of something, but whenever he looked there was nothing to be seen, so he tried an old hunter's trick and turned back around a tree to disguise his intentions."

He paused uncomfortably.

"Out with it, man." I growled. "Look around—it grows late."

"Well, what he says he saw wasn't an animal."

"Native, head hunter?" I queried. Robinson shook his head.

"Well then, confound it." My patience was eroding. "What did Saric think it was?" The jungle was darkening swiftly, and with the thickening mist, the men would be wondering what our intention was.

"Saric said the creature was man-shaped, but looked tall and lean. It was black as the night, without any color. A pair of yellow eyes staring straight at him. It had a tail, and on its head were *horns*…"

Chills crawled down my back as a sudden horror reached out to my heart. The next question was a terrible one, but I had to ask it.

"Robinson, when those two chaps refused to come with us, what exactly did they fear?" I dreaded his answer. Robinson's eyes grew wide.

"They said there was a devil man in the hollow…"

We both looked back at Saric who still had not moved. I told Robinson that camp must be made, but a light one. There would be little sleep tonight. He and Chatra had noticed a small clearing just ahead and were going to suggest this before our pause. I sent him forward and wanted the men to move slowly onward, on full alert. I was not convinced of what Saric had seen, but I knew he had seen something.

As the men resumed the march, I went back to Saric. He very carefully stood up, and pointed towards a thick clump of bushes about forty yards to our rear. I looked intensely but saw nothing. I strained my eyes for at least a minute and then suddenly I spotted a figure.

There was a deeper shadow within the shadows, and I caught a pair of yellow pinpricks—unflinching, gazing directly at us.

My breathing became heavier and I reached for my rifle, never taking my eyes off what we were seeing. As I slowly moved my weapon forward, the eyes vanished and the shadow was gone.

The temptation to fire off a shot into the brush was great, but discretion did not allow for it. The men would be alarmed, and I needed all their resources as intact as possible. In all my experience in the wild, I had never seen such a thing move so quickly and quietly. What had we spotted?

I touched the guide on his shoulder and nodded ahead to where the rest had gone. I did not want to be left too far behind. The two of us headed out but Saric walked facing backwards. He was not going to let himself become exposed to the elusive creature stalking us, so we made our way slowly towards the clearing. When at last we neared it, Robinson and Edward had made sure that we did not get too far back and joined in our progress without speaking.

The trees opened up and there was a decent patch of low grass that was suitable for setting camp. The men had unpacked the bare essentials, and a good sized fire was burning as we entered the area. This was not too far off the path, and we could regain it with ease the next day. The night sky was becoming increasingly difficult to see as the mist did not let up. I wanted four men on watch at all times. There would be no surprises while the others slept, if rest could be found at all.

I wanted either Chatra or Saric awake through dawn at least. Their jungle skills were at levels that none of us outsiders could ever attain to. Neither questioned the order—they realized that we were dealing with an unknown creature here. They spoke for a while in their native tongue and seemed to agree on something. Saric went to one of the camp perimeters and held a rifle in his lap. Edward, Jamie, and Woods posted the other corners, while myself and Robinson held a conference. The other two now lay in repose.

"You saw it then." It was a statement more than question.

I nodded grimly. "Never seen such a strange beast. Didn't get much of a look, just the outline and those penetrating eyes. If I wouldn't know any better, it seemed to be measuring us somehow. Brought my gun to sight, and it disappeared in a flash. Gone in an instant. Anything that can move with such speed is deadly, not to be underestimated."

Robinson could only nod his head in agreement. "Well then, until we know what manner of creature we are dealing with, there can be no lowering of caution while in this hollow. Could be a species undiscovered before. That explains the native's fear. Whether or not it is dangerous we don't know, and hopefully will never find out. Although, one beast against an armed company is at a great disadvantage."

His words made sense, but did little to ease my concerns. True, we did have firepower and a numbers advantage, as long as there did not exist others of the creature, but it was the nature of what we were dealing with that worried me. Probable intelligence, speed and agility, and foremost we were trespassing in its domain. These were all equalizers in the field. I knew not to what side the odds favored. *That* bothered me.

I told Robinson to get some rest, we would both have a chance at watch later. He went off, and I surveyed the camp. The encircling trees were impenetrable in the darkness. My men remained on post, and had weapons ready.

The silence was chilling.

Not a single night bird to be heard. The jungle pressed in on us from all sides waiting to forever swallow up any who dared venture beyond the perimeter of our camp. The air felt heavy and thick with anticipation, the dampness seeping into our clothes. I observed all these things, and realized then that we should never have stepped foot into the hollow.

This valley was somehow unnatural. The world known to us had been left behind. We had been warned and chose to ignore the warning. What price would we have to pay?

Well, I had to at least try to get some sleep. A tired man makes mistakes, and there was no room for any down here in the hollow.

I began to make my way to the fire and glanced over at Saric, and froze instantly. The native now stood and was staring up at the trees in front of himself, raising the sights of his gun. I followed his gaze and saw a pair of yellow, unblinking eyes in the branches. But before I could bring my own weapon around, they vanished. I walked over to Saric as he now was aiming to fire, but there was nothing visible.

Our movements had caught the attention of the others, and they were now looking our way. At that moment the silence was suddenly broken by a bloodcurdling howl from the trees, and everyone sprang to their feet.

A shadowy figure erupted without warning from the jungle opposite Saric and myself, and went directly at Edward. The creature moved with amazing speed as it grabbed the big man and leaped back into the trees carrying him as if he were weightless.

It happened so fast that no one had time to react.

There was a brief scream of anguish and we knew Edward was gone.

Jamie and Woods started firing rounds from their rifles in the general area but there was no more movement or noise.

"Wait, stop firing!" Robinson was bellowing to the men. They were shooting blindly and in near panic. "Hold on!" Chaos took hold for a few moments as the men continued shooting. Robinson ran up to them to restore some order.

As soon as this had taken place, Chatra had picked up a flaming brand and scanned the trees in all directions. Saric never took his eyes off the tree line for a second.

"No firing!" I yelled. "Keep alert for the beast! If we panic now, we are lost!"

Robinson came to my side. "What type of demon is this? I've never seen such speed! It carried Edward off like a sack of flour!"

Chatra yelled over to Robinson for a few seconds. "What does he say?" Robinson's face looked hideously pale in the flickering firelight.

"He thinks this is all a trap. The creature distracted us. It was no accident that it chose Edward. It went after the biggest and strongest of us first."

His words only added to my horror. If this creature had such cunning, there was no way of gauging its next move. The big hunter was taken out so quickly that the shock of it had not sunk in yet.

"Come on, man, pull yourself together." I looked over to see Jamie shaking with terror, and Landers was trying to snap him out of it. Jamie was mumbling incoherently and appeared to be in great distress. Meanwhile, Chatra had thrown numerous flaming branches all around the camp to increase our visibility.

The whole setting had an unreal quality to it. Such a creature should not exist. Could not exist. We were in a living nightmare without waking. There would be no help from the outside world.

A shot suddenly rang out in the night. I lifted my gun and saw Woods firing into the trees. Robinson was also firing, and now Landers was aiming. I wasn't sure what they saw, but hoped they had found a target.

Round after round went off and I scanned the clearing seeing nothing. The two natives moved their rifles up but were looking elsewhere. At this point, Jamie had been forgotten and I saw him staggering apparently in a daze, dangerously close to the brush to the left of Robinson.

"Robinson!" I yelled out over the gunfire but wasn't heard. I started over towards them and now Jamie was only yards from the bushes.

Before my eyes I saw a long vine whip out from between two trees and lassoed around the man's head. He jerked forward like a puppet and flew into the air at least a dozen yards as his neck was broken instantly.

I screamed in rage and fired into the jungle, emptying my rifle.

After several moments, all the firing stopped. Robinson yelled for everyone to hold their weapons and he slowly walked towards the body of Jamie. "Cover me, be alert!" Robinson moved forward in a half crouch, gun ready to fire. He hesitated as he reached Jamie, and pulled him back slowly with one arm.

There was no movement.

I had reloaded and was hoping to catch some glimpse of this monster, but it remained unseen. We all kept our eyes fixed on the jungle, but there was no hint of it anywhere. Our only choice was to wait and pray for sunrise.

One cannot imagine the incredible fear that we faced those dreadful hours until dawn. The cold terror, the shadows we thought we saw, noises we thought we heard. Several times there were shots fired by one of us, and we expected another attack, but none materialized. The creature was temporarily satisfied, but now our number was diminished to six. Who would be the next victim?

As the first ray of light streamed over the jungle canopy, we breathed a little easier. The horror of the night yet lingered—blanketing our minds, shrouding our spirits, but it was time for action. With four still guarding, the rest quickly packed up and we were ready to move. There was no hesitation as we cut straight into the jungle towards the path. Our only chance was to try and leave the hollow as soon as possible in the hope that the creature only came out at nightfall.

Chatra believed that if we followed the trail, we would reach the opposite end of the valley within several hours, so we moved forward at a generous pace. The path led in the direction we felt would bring us out of there, so we continued.

The morning wore on as our group pressed forward through the trees, and as before there was not a sign of any living animal. Now the truth was known. There was no beast alive that would be a match for this deadly predator. It was gaining on midday when I started to wonder if the trail would lead us out. There still was no hint of any incline, and the valley seemed endless. The morning remained uneventful but I wanted to be well out of the hollow by afternoon.

We trudged onward without rest, tired and silent. Everyone shared the same thoughts. There was no need to speak. The events of the previous night had drained us emotionally and physically. Sheer force of will drove us forward.

It was early afternoon when the company halted unexpectedly. I was still in the rear with Saric when the terrain became softer but seemed to have a slight incline. I believed we were nearing the other side at last. The vegetation was incredibly thick here and the path narrowed sharply. A mist started to form around us and the air grew damp. Our visibility decreased sharply when the trackers stopped and called for me to come forward. As I made my way to the front, the brush opened up and I let out a gasp.

In front of us the path abruptly ended into a vast bog with no end in sight, blocking our forward progress. There were several yells of dismay at our predicament, and an uneasy suspicion crept into my head.

"Fool, I am a bloody fool!" I yelled. "All this time we blindly trusted to this trail, never bothering to question the intent of it. Why was it here and who made it? The answer lies before us. That creature is the maker of the path for its own vile purpose, and now has led us to this abysmal swamp!"

The choices which lay before us were grim. We could try and pick our way through it, skirt around the edge, hoping to find an end, or go back through the hollow knowing that we would face another night there.

None of us voted for the last choice so we decided to find a way through the swamp. Within only a few yards from the edge, the footing became treacherous already. Knee-deep in mud, the men tried to find a means of passage out of the murky waters.

The fog was thickening now that we were at the source, and it swirled lazily between the dead tree trunks that had fallen victim to the unquenchable thirst of the bog. Unseen insects droned in the distance, an occasional bullfrog croaked across the dismal fen, as if in mockery of our plight. I could just make out the back of Woods in front me when we came across an area of deep mud that reached our thighs. If this were to become any deeper, we would be forced to turn back.

I yelled up to Woods to check with the trackers and make sure the mud did not get deeper. After a minute he told me to bear to the right where the going was easier. The slime was now up to my midsection and I began to sink lower.

Quicksand!

"Woods!" I yelled. "Rope, now!" He yelled up to the others and they turned back to help. The soft mud did not allow for faster action and I knew better than to struggle, although I was immersed up past my waist now and still sinking. I had forgotten about Saric when I heard a short cry in back of me.

The guide was chest deep in the mire and looking frantically for something to grab onto. There was an old tree half submerged several yards from him but just out of reach. His situation looked desperate.

"Hurry there! Saric is trapped!" The men took their rope out and Woods now retrieved it, but his progress was hampered by the deep mud. Saric was in a panic now, and this only made his situation worse.

"Hold, man! Don't move!" I tried to calm him down but he was overcome with fear. Woods threw out a length of rope to me but was off mark. My own predicament was worsening and I continued sinking. Again Woods tossed the rope and this time I grabbed the end.

He tugged and I didn't budge. Landers was almost at his side now, and looking back I could only see Saric's head. There was not much time left. Landers helped to pull and now Robinson was there as well. The men had to stay back unless they were to share our fate. They needed firmer footing for leverage. I yelled encouragement to Saric but his arms flailed wildly about, his head tilted to keep from swallowing the mud.

The three men now were slowly pulling me out and I was gasping for air as they dragged me through the sludge. When I was out far enough, Robinson came towards me and Woods threw the rope towards Saric, but it was too late.

We watched hopelessly as his right arm hovered over the surface for an instant, then vanished into the depths of the swamp...

Chatra had not said a word, but his eyes betrayed the bitter loss of his kinsman. The rest of us were in great despair—exhausted, frightened, hungry, and not knowing when the swamp would end. We went ahead a bit where more solid ground was to be found and rested.

I felt an odd sensation on my leg and found a huge black leech beneath my pants, blood seeping from my skin. I cut the foul parasite out with my knife and Robinson said "I guess there is life down here anyway." I spat in disgust.

"You know, that mud swallowed us up so quickly, we scarcely had time to react. The experience I've learned with quicksand is patience and do not struggle. That mire went against everything I know. Poor Saric didn't have a prayer."

"This hollow has its own laws," answered Landers. "What we have seen so far defies explanation. Does our guide have any idea of our whereabouts?" Robinson conversed with the taciturn native and replied. "He is unsure of the direction. The mist and swamp have distorted his tracking skills. His choice would be to go where the ground seems more solid, and believes that would take us further north. I agree, and the sooner the better. The day grows old."

His statement brought back our earlier fears and off we went.

The footing began to improve and maybe luck would lead us out yet. Our spirits began to rise as we reached solid ground and left the swamp behind us. But we were still oblivious as to where the valley ended.

Our progress increased and the vegetation was less oppressive on this side. The mist was still with us but not quite as thick. We were in the same twilight since late that morning, and darkness would fall early unless we could reach some higher ground. I called for a short break and Chatra was convinced that the region was starting to level upwards. Finishing quickly, our group made off and we could see that nightfall was nearly upon us as the light was dimming.

We had changed formation now with Robinson walking behind me since the loss of Saric. He had insisted on it and we all stayed close, in single file and everyone within a few yards of each other. The ground had definitely begun sloping upward and we finally reached the bottom edge of the valley. The last reservoir of our strength was being tapped as we knew the end was within sight.

The trees opened up and there before us was the cliff side, but much steeper than we had anticipated. Rocks and boulders were strewn all around and the footing looked treacherous.

I grimly told the men to spread out to reduce the risk of us all being caught in a fall, and up we went. The ascent called for extreme caution, as the ground was loose with numerous rocks and jagged edges all about. A cluster of large boulders lay about a hundred yards above us, and beyond that was a thick area of brambles and high brush before the cliff leveled off.

Darkness had fallen and we were nearing the rocks when Landers let out a curse. Looking up, we spotted a black figure standing among the rock pile, eyes glittering bright yellow.

The creature stood motionless for a moment and then sprang onto an outcropping of huge boulders several dozen yards directly above us. I knew what it had in mind and with an immense show of power it loosened two huge rocks that started tumbling down upon us.

We all tried to scatter but there was no time. One of the boulders headed straight at Robinson, barely missing myself. He was hit square on and toppled helplessly beneath it down the cliff.

Another one passed between Woods and Landers, and they narrowly avoided it. Landers flattened against the ground but Woods was not so fortunate. The movement to avoid being crushed made him lose balance and he fell downwards. I watched as he rolled sideways over and over again, battering against the sharp rocks.

He didn't stop until he was near the bottom and there he remained unmoving.

In all the mayhem, Chatra was the only one to take action. He had continued up to the rock pile with his rifle in hand. I watched as he came within yards of the creature, which now made no attempt to seek cover. I yelled for him to hold his ground and not get too close, and I brought up my gun to aim. The creature stood still, and I could see its unblinking gaze fixed on the native. Chatra pointed his sights on the beast and in that second it chose to move.

With startling agility, it leaped to the right and crouched on top of a large rock formation. Chatra squeezed off several rounds but the monster was already in action. I could not shoot for fear of hitting the guide, so I watched what ensued in horror.

The creature again leaped but this time closer to the tough native, and Chatra whipped out his long knife. The beast feinted left, and then in a blur of lightning speed closed on the hapless man and gave him a crushing blow to the skull. It picked up the unconscious victim and dashed him onto the rocks below.

Enraged, I fired at the demon, and found a target at last. One of my shots struck it in the chest and it howled its hatred at me. It fell on one clawed limb, and I unloaded the rest of my stock, connecting several more times.

Down it fell, and the eyes dimmed. In its last breath, it screamed in such anguish that I nearly collapsed right there. I lay on the ground, still not believing that the beast was dead. I crawled forward and confirmed my hopes. It lay there lifeless, an unknown form of creature that leant substance to the native folklore, and with good reason.

I peered down to the bottom of the cliff trying to make out the body of Woods—but where was Landers? I caught a glimpse of him trying to reach Woods, but now he was gone as well. Maybe he would appear at the top of the cliff, waiting for me.

Woods might yet be alive, although how badly injured I dared not think. I made my way carefully in the dark and found him laying there, and my worst fears were realized. The only thing left for me now was to get out of the hollow and reach the village, but without my men, although I still hoped to find Landers. I sobbed and cursed our ill fortune, but there was nothing I could do to ease my anguish.

As I started upwards, a noise broke the silence that froze every nerve in my body. A blood-curdling howl echoed through the night, coming *down* from the cliff.

There was another creature.

The final shred of my hope vanished as it was answered by another scream, this one coming from the jungle. There were several of these monsters, and they had come to avenge their fallen brethren.

And now I hear a howl much closer in the trees behind me, and I can sense its presence as it hunts me. My rifle is empty and all I have left is my hunting knife, which is useless against such a demon.

All I have time for is regret as I await the approach of my enemy...

WHERE TRAILS SOMETIMES LEAD

A passing shadow fleets by. Elusive phantom? Merely a woodland animal scampering for cover. Creaking steps, flapping shutters, what diabolical entity lurks? It's just the wind. Fiery streaks across a winter sky. Otherworldly beings? Terrestrial sources, natural or man-made. Imagination is the largest creator of the unknown and sinister, our own inner demons awakened as human fantasy coaxed from oblivion, molded into possibility, and breathed tangible existence. Explainable. But sometimes not...

The late autumn sun melted beneath a rage of dark gray clouds rolling over the wooded hills of the New Jersey Pine Barrens, whispering of a premature twilight.

Marvin sat before the vintage wooden desk in the cozy office of his rancher, dressed against the seasonal chill in a green flannel shirt and faded blue jeans. He stared outside at the mischievous fall scene, across the forests bordering his property and beyond. His eyes of blue sea-ice gazed over tree tops while his mind fidgeted with a message left on his answering machine. One lean finger tapped absently against the partially open drawer, and he caught himself daydreaming.

The weather forecast predicted a restless night—a good time to stay indoors, but curiosity was such an unpredictable, peculiar thing, prodding incessantly at the psyche once piqued. He picked up the phone receiver, clicking the pads to a familiar number. Several rings.

More.

Someone spoke from the other end—a husky voice, deep but casual. "Hello, Marvin. What's up?"

"Hi Greg. Hey, he called back this afternoon."

"Um…Mr. Harris?"

"Yeah. Left an interesting, no…strange message on my answering machine." Marvin snatched a memo notepad from the near corner of his desk. On it were scribbled numbers and directions.

"What did he say?" Greg's voice grew a bit higher in tone.

"Basically that we should see him ASAP. Seems he found something remarkable, although he didn't leave me any details." Marvin's voice was laced with a suggestion of disappointment, and excitement as well.

"Hmm." Greg paused on the other end. "He has me wondering now…when do you want to check him out? Saturday, maybe? We'll get a few of the others to tag along, I can make some calls then."

Marvin hesitated. "Actually, I was thinking tonight, you and me going over."

A low chuckle. "You don't want to mess around, do you? Let me think…Staci is going shopping, Ricky has band practice—but he can get a ride home from school. Yeah, I can swing it, I guess. But they're calling for possible storms."

"I heard that too. But I *really* want to see this guy. Just something in his voice, you know? Like he's not full of crap, or some wacko groupie. When I talked to him, I felt that he genuinely believed he'd found some hard evidence. More than footprints, or just some strange sounds in the woods. We have enough of *that* all the time…"

"I know what you mean. All right, I'll be over within the hour."

"Great. I'll drive." Marvin nodded to himself.

"See ya' soon."

Click.

Marvin rubbed the day-old growth on his chin, brushed a lock of brown hair from his fortyish face. He was definitely excited. But that's why he researched the supernatural. It was the thrill of the chase, he admitted to himself. And the rare moments when fact and fiction blurred, possibilities emerging. Harris had sounded eager, although somewhat cautious. A strange blend of emotions. Regardless, the man had devoted over a decade of his life to local folklore. And he now lived within arm's reach of the Forked River Mountain region, where legend lay dormant, waiting to be discovered or disproved. Or maybe just waiting…

Like-minded men they were—himself, Greg, and several others, all feeling the same incessant compulsion. Searching for the truth. There were other groups scattered about the state, amateurs and serious hunters alike. All looking for the same thing.

Marvin stood, turning off his desk lamp.

The room was already a haven for shadows impatient for nightfall. He peered outside, his gaze sweeping the gentle slope of grass that plunged a hundred yards into oblivion, a forest of mixed hardwoods looming reverently nearby, a touch of the magical brushing against a small presence of men and women living beneath the sanctity of reachable wilderness. Marvin wanted so much to be in communion with these woods which he held sacred, choosing his home for this very reason.

And the trees always suggested more to him, an aura of secrecy. Mystery. What really lay inside those vast depths, beyond the vision of man? He wanted to know. *Needed* to know. A natural passion, it bordered on obsession at times. To find the secrets, prove their existence. Especially for one in particular.

The Jersey Devil.

<<<—>>>

The Explorer grinded along the country road, sharing the evening with few vehicles. Homes were sparse—not many were located this close to the hills. The occasional twinkling of quiet lights told Marvin they were still within 'civilized' areas, and this notion played on his fancy in polarizing fashion. It was comfortable knowing that people were never far away—it was, after all, New Jersey. But in another sense, he longed for that twinge of isolation, even living within the Garden State. There remained countless miles of unpopulated lands where man was a stranger, and the wild still held reign. And secrets.

"Almost there?" Greg glanced over at him.

The presence of his friend was always another comfort to Marvin. Like the scattered houses, Greg was a bastion of security, a concrete foundation. He also acted as constant reminder for practical thinking, always preaching to Marvin of mundane explanations when he tended to stray. And at times he was certainly guilty of such, over zealousness shrouding logic. Greg's input was invaluable, considering they tried to approach their elusive quarry with sound reasoning and firm footing.

"Should be around the next bend." Marvin gripped the wheel tighter and leaned forward in his seat, squinting in the fading light. "Said the mailbox was clearly marked, and then a stone driveway. A long one," he added.

Greg pointed. "There it is, I think."

His friend shifted, adjusting his seat belt. The man appeared bearish, his large frame looking too big even for the sizable SUV. A collegiate athletic standout, his American dream of becoming a professional football player had shattered along with his kneecap in the last game of his senior year. He still retained a slight limp. Greg remained intimidating though—wide, hulking shoulders with a bull's neck. Stark black hair added severity to his already impressive physique, although the clean-cut face and chiseled looks gave him the boy-next-door look, softening his overall impression.

Marvin turned the vehicle, heading towards a dim lane. "That's it," he said. They plunged into a dense forest of native trees—ancient oaks, red cedars, and the ever-present pines. Stones crackled beneath the tires, and numerous twigs lay along the road. "Harris lives back this way, at least two miles, he told me. No neighbors within a half-dozen more."

Greg reached into the backseat, rummaging through a small bag. They always came prepared, even when interviewing people. Their so-called 'survival' packs included a tape recorder, drinking canteen filled with spring water, compass, maps, camera (with extra battery), and other useful items while out on a search. You never knew where a lead could end up, and from experience, they came primed for anything. More than once they'd walked off into the forest as an eager eyewitness showed them purported evidence of the mysterious creature. And mostly it ended in vague markings, assignable to almost anything native to the Pine Barrens. But once in a while they were not disappointed, returning with optimism and unanswered questions...

They continued rumbling up the road for several minutes, the landscape never changing. Endless waves of trees marched beside them, and Marvin couldn't shake the feeling of being swallowed by the expansive New Jersey heartland. The feeling invigorated and unsettled him at the same time. It always did. He knew they must be nearing the man's house, and wondered again what he'd found. Marvin felt a knot of anxiety, fervently wishing it would prove important.

He snapped his head quickly to the left as a darker shadow moved between the trees. His foot reflexively tapped the brakes, and Greg shot him a puzzled look.

"What's the matter?"

Marvin slowed the vehicle. "I don't know, thought I saw something..." He scanned the dark maw of the forest, eyes searching for movement. After a few seconds, he shook his head. "Probably nothing. Excitement, maybe."

"Hmm. Can't blame you. These woods can creep you out. I've felt the same way before, especially out on a hunt. Like that time in August, around the lake?" Greg pursed his lips. "Weird, like there was something with us that evening."

Marvin agreed. "I remember. And Cindy practically ran all the way back to the cars." He chuckled. "But there was a strange feeling that time, and the noises—far away, but always the same distance somehow."

Greg coughed. "Giving me the chills just thinking about it..."

"Two grown men, afraid of the bogeyman." Marvin sighed, concentrating on the narrow road ahead.

"And maybe that's what this is really all about, when you think about it." Greg's voice grew quiet. "What people fear the most—things walking the night. Compelling us onwards, out of our own curiosity...and fear," he added.

Marvin arched an eyebrow. "That's an interesting spin. We challenge our own terror instead of hiding it and burying the fear away. A lot of people joke, say it's all a bunch of crap. But you know what? I bet a lot of them are the most *terrified* of all, and will never admit it."

As Marvin finished his sentence a clearing broke in front of them, a small log cabin jutting outwards from the twilight. Trees and thickets surrounded the structure on all sides with a smaller building to the back. The sight made him feel uneasy for a moment, as if he'd wandered into another land, a strange and uncomfortable world. Log cabin or gingerbread house? He chided himself. He really *was* nervous tonight...

"Here we are," Greg said, unbuckling his seat belt and grabbing the supply bag from behind him. Parking the truck, Marvin stretched, then both men gathered their belongings and stepped out.

Despite being sheltered by the woods, a brisk wind slapped Marvin's face, and the tree branches swayed restlessly around them. Dried leaves scuttled over the rough lawn, the grass evenly cut although bare and mossy in spots. The moon had already climbed into the sky, but was only a brighter shadow as the clouds greedily smothered it. The air smelled like rain.

They walked up to the front porch, modestly-sized with a single wooden rocker, its texture a perfect match with the cedar siding. Several metal lanterns swung gently from long nails embedded into the porch rafters, all of them lighted.

"Looks like we've been expected." Greg gestured with his thumb towards the lamps. "But I thought you didn't get back to him earlier, right?"

Marvin shook his head, lightly rapping on the door. "No. We only talked twice before, actually. Nothing that I haven't told you already. Just about his research, our interest, not much else…"

There was no answer, and the cabin appeared dark, no light illuminating the interior, and the single window was shuttered. They waited for another minute and Greg retreated to the edge of the porch, glancing at the sky. He then went to the side, angling his neck and peering around back. "Hello!" he shouted, his voice sounding muffled against the growing wind. "Mr. Harris?"

Marvin continued knocking, even trying the door handle, but it was heavily bolted.

Silence.

Greg frowned. "There's a pickup around back, but he might have another vehicle."

"Maybe." Marvin joined him. "But he specifically said he would be around until at least Sunday, then he was supposed to visit a friend in Trenton. About his recent find." He muttered to himself. "I wish he would have told me more…"

"Wait, maybe he's in that other building." Greg leaped over the low rail, still possessing great physical abilities in spite of his college injuries. The man was a very durable forty-two year old, and maintained his excellent conditioning.

Marvin joined him, taller and leaner than his friend but capable himself. "Come to think of it, he did mention a workshop. That's where he's probably at right now."

The pair walked alongside the cabin, stepping over a path made of round wood blocks, the gaps filled in with crushed driveway rock. The pickup sat directly on top of a packed stone bedding with the smaller building behind it, basically a one-story workshop, roughly the size of a single garage. Marvin noticed that from the back of the cabin hung additional lanterns and heavy shutters barred each window. Folklore memories teased him about the significance of such, but he ignored this prodding, although it gave him the impression that Harris desired privacy. Perhaps security. That line of thought disturbed him more, and he wondered who would bother the man out here. There were no homes within a few miles driving distance at least, the bordering country edging the very heart of the Pine Barrens, reserved and unoccupied land. Natural caution of course, he mused. Probably kept firearms as well.

All the lanterns were lit though—a good indication that Harris was nearby, on the immediate grounds, if not in the buildings themselves.

They reached the workshop, finding another pair of lanterns dangling above the doorway. A window faced them, and the rest of the structure was solid wood. Greg opened the screen door, then knocked.

Marvin whistled, but it sounded ineffectual against the mournful wind. Greg called out, shaking his head. "Where did the guy go? He should have heard us by now. That cabin is small, and there doesn't seem to be any basement. Let's see here…"

He tried the knob, and it turned easily in his grip. They locked eyes, and Marvin gestured forward with his head.

"Hello, Mr. Harris?" Greg pushed the door open, speaking apologetically. Marvin followed him inside, letting the screen door gently close. A splash of smoky light from a kerosene lantern illuminated the interior of a tight, but well-kept work room. The lamp sat on a rectangular table, which was filled with an assortment of notepads and utensils. Two racks rested against opposite walls, containers and outdoor supplies placed neatly on the shelves.

"Well, he's not in here, that's for sure." Greg examined the items, careful not to touch anything. "I feel a bit like a trespasser, but we *were* at least invited…"

"Yeah." Marvin was puzzled, and he flopped down on the single chair in front of the table. On a whim, he snatched the cell phone out from his trouser pocket. "Saved his number…" he responded to Greg's curious stare. "In case he's in the house."

A moment later Marvin scowled. "No service, I should have known." He looked over the array of items laying on the table, a large piece of graph paper catching his attention. "Hmm, looks like a map."

Greg walked over to him. "Did he refer to anything in particular?"

Marvin shrugged. "Harris said he took meticulous notes, trying to zero in on what he called the 'hot spots' of activity."

"Nothing unusual there. Same thing we do, putting all the clues and stories together, trying to formulate any patterns." Greg leaned over his shoulder.

"Right. Harris claimed to really be onto something, though. He made a reference to the geography in this area, points of magnetic strength, stuff like that. When he first called me, I remember him saying that he was getting close—damn close he actually said." Marvin examined the paper, realizing with mild surprise that it included the cabin and its surroundings.

"Close to what? Finding proof of the Jersey Devil?" Greg raised the wick on the lantern.

"Exactly," Marvin replied. He bent closer to the map, noticing the description of an area marked in bold red. Chills snaked up his spine as he read the script to himself.

Clearly written was a single word.

Lair.

«‹‹—››»

Thunder cracked outside the workshop, and Marvin snapped his head up in alarm.

"Jumpy…" Greg smirked at him, then his face became serious. "Storm's rolling in, might get pretty nasty. What do you want to do?"

Marvin didn't feel right about leaving without knowing where Harris was. And what if something had happened to the man? He looked down at the map again. There were numerous points marked on the graph, numbers measuring various things, such as barometric pressure, elevation, magnetic readings. "Seems like Harris has developed some type of scientific approach, but what's really interesting are these marks. Especially *this* one. He pointed them out to Greg, who seemed confused.

"The lair? Of what—the Jersey Devil?" He gave a short laugh. "Now that would be a real kicker. But I seriously doubt it. No one's ever made such a claim before, except maybe around the Leeds house. And that's a haul from here." Greg paused for a second. "Look. He's drawn a series of trails leading from behind his property. Don't know what to make of it all. Maybe he's in this thing way too deep…"

Marvin thought about it. He knew the obsession he himself felt at times. But never had it affected his personal life. More like a hunger for knowledge. Sure, it caused some late nights reading and on the web, a few annoyed comments from his wife, but she was all right with his hobby, even if it was a bit strange.

"How far away is it…according to the map?" Greg rubbed his chin. "Maybe we should go looking for Harris. Something might have happened to him."

"You're reading my mind." Marvin stood up. "I was thinking the same thing. All alone out here. He might very well be out on a late afternoon hike. Weather crept up on him. I don't know…" His voice drifted off.

Greg leaned close, whispering. "Maybe the Jersey Devil got him."

Marvin frowned. "I didn't say *that.*"

Greg patted his arm. "I know you didn't. Hey, I'm as curious as you are, but I still think it's just some weird-looking bird."

The wind howled as the storm lashed out in growing fury. Both men turned around, startled as a large shadow loomed before the doorway.

Something was outside.

«« — »»

A flash of lightning illuminated a tall silhouette, hovering motionless before the entrance. The mesh of the screen was painted in an eerie silver sheen, reflected off the sporadic bolts streaking across the background sky. A tense moment ensued as both men looked warily into the night, their fears surfacing, the stories and rumors taking the form of ghastly possibility as they found themselves isolated and confused by circumstance.

The figure moved forward into the hazy light.

Wide eyes matched their own surprised gaze, white hair ruffled by the agitated wind. It was a man, looking close to seventy. Harris…

"Wow. Scared us." Marvin moved forward, arms raised in greeting. "We looked all over for you, thought something might have happened. Door was open and we came inside. I'm Marvin, and this is Greg." He offered his hand.

Without speaking, Harris pushed his way inside, quickly glancing over his shoulder, the pronounced gesture sending a chill along Marvin's spine. Harris closed both doors behind him, turning the bolt on the inner panel.

"Is that necessary?" Greg asked good-naturedly, but Harris ignored the remark and came further into the light, collapsing onto the chair. It was then that Marvin noticed the large brown sack he held beneath the crook of one arm. Harris sat there in silence for several long moments, the two men exchanging cautious looks. Uncomfortable, Marvin attempted to break the tension with a question, but Harris cut him short.

"Things have happened since I called you."

"Like what? Have you found something else?" Marvin examined the man's clothes. Soiled trousers, tall boots caked with mud, insulated gray flannel shirt torn in several spots, pieces of leaves and small twigs stuck on the material. He'd obviously been out on his own expedition, and Marvin was now doubly curious as to why the man was acting so strange.

Harris nodded. "Searching for answers. A passion of mine. Thought the same as you did. Not anymore." He peered up at them, slowly looking from one to the next. His face was wintry, unshaven. Pale. Marvin noticed his hands trembled, but whether from illness or fear, he could only guess...

Greg interjected. "You called Marvin, told him you found something interesting. We happened to see the charts sitting on the table. Can you explain this to us?"

"Don't know if I want to anymore. Questions for riddles..." His voice drifted. "Some things are best left to themselves. And I'm afraid for what I've found." Harris was genuinely alarmed, and with every gust of wind, he snapped his head around, eyes blinking nervously at the door. He stood, checking the window and securing the lock.

"Look." Marvin started, then paused, trying to find the proper words. "If you're in some kind of trouble, tell us what we can do to help. We came all the way out here on our own. Believe me, you didn't drag us against our will. We're researchers, hunters. Maybe a little nuts ourselves, but it's a passionate hobby."

Greg frowned at Marvin's choice of words, despite his friend's honest intentions.

"I'm *not* crazy." Harris retorted. "Let's make damn sure of that. But I don't want to put you in any danger, so I'll have to ask you to leave. Now."

Greg raised his hands, placing them palms upward in confusion. "He didn't mean to offend you, Mr. Harris."

"I know, but I'm sorry." Harris looked down at the sack. "I've brought something on myself, and deeply regret it. Take my advice—let things be. Forget all about the Jersey Devil. And me."

Marvin and Greg were bewildered by the man's odd behavior, but there seemed little choice left for them. Harris clearly was disturbed and wanted them gone.

"All right, but I'm sorry you feel this way. I apologize for the intrusion." Marvin waved to Greg and they walked towards the doorway.

"I'll follow you out with the lamp." They hesitated, waiting for Harris as he picked up the sack and grabbed the lantern.

Greg was closest to the door and he fumbled with the bolt. They were all startled as a loud *thump* came from overhead, and Harris snapped at Greg. "Don't unlock it."

The three men froze, all of them staring at the ceiling. Marvin felt a terrible sense of dread clutching at his chest.

Greg scowled. "Just a tree branch…"

It sounded again. Louder.

Marvin's entire body tingled with fear. He looked at Harris, whose face was a ghostly white.

"What the *hell* did you find out there…"

《《—》》

The three men stood in nervous silence for long moments, Harris unwilling to speak, Marvin waiting for an answer to his question. An answer he might not want to hear or believe. The mood was intense and even Greg fidgeted uncertainly. Marvin looked hard at Harris. His eyes reflected surprise, but more powerful was the fear lurking inside the murky orbs.

It was Greg who finally broke the spell. "Just the wind, like I said. Let's go." He again moved to open the bolt.

"Wait." Marvin's voice was low, but the tone was unmistakable. It was a request that Greg couldn't refuse, out of the close friendship the two maintained. "I have a bad feeling about this." He angled his head towards their frightened host. "Harris, you owe us an explanation—we came all the way out here. And you're obviously upset about something."

The wind moaned outside. Rain pelted the workshop.

Greg opened his mouth to speak, then thought better of it. Marvin

95

felt sweat beneath his shirt, cold and uncomfortable. Harris trembled. Tension grew, emerging from the shell of their ignorance and confusion. Invisible fingers probed, reaching into their psyche and tweaking the nightmares from slumber, breathing life into what had been only possibility, and merging with whatever waited outside, real or imagined.

Marvin swallowed, his throat parched and constricted.

"It feeds on our fear." Harris croaked the words.

"I'm not afraid of the storm, or a stray animal. Probably just a branch anyway." Greg was quick to respond, but his normally confident face was clouded in doubt.

"That sack. Something inside. It's responsible, isn't it?" Marvin pointed to the bag in accusation. Harris reluctantly nodded.

"What did you *find?*"

Harris cowered, slumping into the chair. "Proof." He lowered his voice, and the men drew closer to listen.

"Found its lair...or where it comes from."

Nothing moved overhead.

Harris whispered. "My calculations led me there. Not too far away. All those years of searching, I never dreamed I would find it practically in my own backyard." He gestured vaguely to the rear of the building.

"Wait..." Greg leaned towards him. "You claim to have found where the Jersey Devil lives? Is that right?"

"No." Harris shook his head. "It's *nothing* like that. Not some monster living in a lake, or haunting a patch of woods. Foolishness."

Marvin frowned at Greg. His back felt like ice, and he silently wished that whatever was on the roof had left. He tried not to think about it.

"Then what?" Greg stared at the sack impatiently.

"I don't entirely understand myself. Only a guess—that's all." Harris rubbed dried fingers together nervously. "The elements, nature. We know so little..." He looked up at the ceiling. "Sometimes, things go wrong. Places rub against each other, it ain't natural at all."

Marvin was now totally confused. Greg interrupted. "You're not making much sense. Can you explain what all this has to do with anything?"

"Worlds touch, things happen." Harris nodded to himself, his voice drifting even lower. "Things cross over..."

His words filled Marvin with a terrible sense of foreboding. The tightness in his chest felt painful, and his stomach roiled in discontent.

"I'll *show* you."

Harris reached for the sack, untying the strings, and they watched him expectantly. He pulled out an object, and Marvin had never felt more terrified in his life. Greg gasped.

On the table sat a large rock, smooth and colorless. Embedded, actually fossilized inside of the rock, were tiny airplanes, the era unmistakably mid-century. The detail was incredibly real. *Too* real to be anything other than authentic...

Marvin leaned nearer, staggered by the sight of this fantastic object, his mind reeling with impossibilities. Fear coursed through his veins, clutching at his throat and tearing down the walls of his understanding, leaving him uncomfortably mired in something closer to a waking nightmare. And it became much worse as the next revelation crushed down upon him.

For within the airplanes were the miniature forms of men.

《《——》》

The air in the small workshop felt stifling, and Marvin's head swam in unreality. His entire body was encased, trapped inside of an invisible, frozen shroud of uncertainty.

Impossible.

Madness. A trick. Reason played against his senses. Fought for control of his sanity. Explanations repeated themselves inside his mind, a litany of words attempting to banish anything but a normal, logical, scientific approach to what lay before him.

Greg was stunned into silence. He moved as if to touch the rock, then hesitated, withdrawing his hand. Harris shook his head quickly in response. "I wouldn't—you're already drawn into this. How far, I don't yet know...Best to leave it alone, and forget what I've told you and what you've seen."

"*Where* the hell did you get this? I'm not going anywhere until I know more." Marvin's eyes glimmered as curiosity quenched his fear and hesitation.

The older man shifted uneasily. "Seems like you won't listen to reason then." He muttered to himself.

"We don't know what to think," Greg added, folding his arms. "Or what to believe."

Harris shot him a withering glance. "I warned you, I tried."

Greg looked at his friend, and Marvin shrugged. "We're investigators, and you've shown us something incredible. How can you expect us to just walk away?"

"For your own good. Don't forget what's out there." Harris pointed towards the window, and Greg scowled. "Let's find out then…"

Marvin held up a hand. "I'm not convinced of anything, Greg. But this needs some explanation—it's just too unbelievable. We're close to something, but I sure don't know what. And how is this connected to the Jersey Devil?"

"You've found it." Harris placed the rock back inside the sack. "It knows about me, of course. I think it's tolerated my presence as I hunted for it even. But I've passed that point now by taking this."

The two men listened to his low voice, and outside the storm was silent, hunkering patiently down. And maybe something else with it as well…

The old man's voice was hushed. "A series of caves. Not on any map. The land is peculiar there, dark and cool. Quiet. Animals seem to avoid it, birds stay clear. I heard strange noises. Found odd signs. One year ago, shortly after I moved here. And then I saw the *haze*."

His eyes grew unfocused, and Marvin swallowed heavily, drawn in by the man's tale.

Harris continued. "A weird shimmering. The land is always foggy there, and sunlight fails to break through. When I first walked beneath the ancient pines, I knew there was something special about it." He faltered for a moment, trying to find proper words. "Hard to explain, but I felt like I was near something incredible, powerful. The hair on my arms would stand up at times, my equipment never seemed to work. Pictures came out blurred. And then I saw it…"

Rain blasted against the building, causing Marvin to jump, and Greg looked up.

Harris whispered. "A shadow within the shadows. Too large to be anything I could identify, its shape was…weird. And I caught only a quick glimpse, before nightfall. I never stayed out there after dark. Never. Too afraid."

"What did you see?" Marvin knelt on one knee, his face inches away from the older man's.

"A creature beyond understanding. I knew what it was right then. Looked liked a mixture of several animals—horse, bat, horns on the small head. It was the Jersey Devil…"

"Did it approach you?" Greg's voice sounded cautious. Neutral.

"It watched me, for a few seconds. Then winged off into the brush. My heart pounded, I thought I was going to collapse out there in that forsaken forest. And *that* in itself was a terrible thought."

"And the rock?" Marvin gestured towards the sack.

Harris rubbed his chin. "That one came by a stroke of luck, two days ago when I called you. I had to tell someone else, someone who wouldn't just take me for an old fool. I needed to prove that I really *wasn't* going crazy. Inside a dense grove, sprawled against foothills, the mist was thick and heavy. I stumbled on some loose rock and spotted an opening. A small cave."

He passed a trembling hand through his thin hair before speaking again. "I crawled through, enough room to permit a large man. Scanned the interior and saw a series of other passages. Took one of them, wondering if I should venture in by myself. Curiosity over discretion. I noticed that odd sensation again, a static charge of sorts. And then before my eyes the air shimmered, glittering like a veil. It happened only for a second, so quick that I didn't realize what was going on. That's when I saw the rock."

Marvin didn't know what to think. The story was bizarre, Harris was strange…chills scurried along his arms—and the night outside was unfriendly. He didn't forget about the noise on the roof. What had really caused it?

His friend continued pressing the man. "It needs to be examined. I can't explain what it is, but someone can." Greg shook his head in wonder.

"I think I might understand…" Harris looked at his own hands. "It's a mixture, a freak occurrence. Planes, and the pilots, caught in some incomprehensible event. A collision of worlds, dimensions maybe. The fabric of matter distorted, the result something *unbelievable*."

Marvin gasped. "The Jersey Devil—you think it's related to what you found then?"

"Yes!" Harris slapped the table, his eyes sparkling with emotion. "A hybrid creature. Unique. Think about it, an assortment of different species, combined together from being caught within this crack of reality. Horse, goat, bat maybe, and human…"

His words were chilling. Marvin felt numb, his mind racing at the extraordinary theory. Greg was silent, lost in his own thoughts.

Harris spoke louder, more confident. "Intelligent. A blend of nature, united into a singular entity. It fits all the legendary descriptions."

"That's horrifying. But it kind of makes sense…if it *does* actually exist." Marvin slowly nodded to himself.

"Of course it exists!" Harris snapped at him with conviction. "This passion drove you out here. You know the truth as well—it's in your heart."

Marvin looked hard at him, and then Greg, but his friend offered nothing in return, only a confused stare.

"And maybe it's happened before." Harris raised a finger. "Look at the history of man, the folklore and mythology. Beasts of legend, bearing the marks and characteristics of diverse animals. The stuff of nightmares, spawned in truth. And within the Pine Barrens there exists one of these doorways. Maybe it was always here, maybe not. I think they might be temporary. Unpredictable."

"Why would the creature linger nearby then?" Greg asked.

Harris appeared genuinely sad. "To guard this rift so nothing else gets caught maybe?"

"Or comes through…" Marvin instantly regretted *that* line of thought. Greg and Harris both stared at him.

"That's certainly a horrible notion. I haven't even considered that one." Harris mumbled to himself, shivering quickly.

Greg breathed deeply. "Another idea. The thing might be in torment, hoping to reverse the process that created it. Searching to regain its humanity. But what a terrible fate…"

All three of them were silenced by Greg's powerful statement. Marvin felt an incredible sense of pity and horror at his friend's theory. Could it be possible that the Jersey Devil was sentient, perhaps highly intelligent, endlessly waiting to revert back into its former human existence? But it may even have been created from several different species. And he doubted such an incredible series of events could ever be changed or duplicated. A perdition of madness and horror…

"Well, it's all just speculation at this point." Harris stood. "But it followed me—that much I do know. Saw something from the corner of my eye, hopping from tree to tree, just a vague silhouette. Thought it was my imagination…wish it were. I hurried back this evening after returning to the cave, and here we are. So I know I wasn't dreaming about finding *this* at least." He gingerly patted the sack.

"And what makes you think we're in any danger?" Marvin folded his arms.

Harris replied. "I went there earlier, and that thing followed me back. Maybe it was content to just let me snoop before, and there's no record of anyone being actually harmed by it that we know of...but *this* is here now."

They all stared at the bag.

The storm raged outside, the wind gaining strength.

"It could be angry. I took that rock, maybe I've gone too far..."

His voice trailed off ominously, and then a tremendous crack of thunder pummeled the workshop, sending them all sprawling to the floor.

«««—»»»

"A lightning strike."

Greg was the first to speak as they stumbled around, shaken by the powerful vibration. "Too damn close for comfort," he added nervously.

Marvin regained his footing, helping Harris to the chair. They both looked up fearfully. The older man's eyes raked across the ceiling.

Something...

Then they heard it. A noise began which chilled them all. A slight scratching against the wood. It originated from above, working its way slowly around. Towards the middle of the building, then stopping.

Circling.

Silence.

"Do you believe me now?" His voice was stricken, his earlier terror taking hold once more. "It's here..."

Greg peered at the ceiling doubtfully, locking stares with his friend. But Marvin was convinced that something lurked outside. Something intelligent, perhaps malevolent, and utterly beyond their comprehension. The quiet was terrible and they waited there for long, tense moments.

Without warning a hideous yell pierced the night and awakening their worst nightmares, immediately followed by a loud crunching sound. Pieces of wood and plaster dropped down on them as the roof began to give way.

"Out!" Greg yelled, going for the door and pointing at Marvin to grab Harris. The older man snatched the bag, and Greg worked the lock open. In swift succession they rushed into the night, greeted by nasty shafts of rain and slapped wickedly by a cold autumn wind. Marvin looked skyward, terrified at what he might see above them. Great arcs of lightning slashed across the sky, illuminating huge storm clouds. Trees whipped and creaked, thrashed about by the relentless weather. The entire forest looked threatening, appearing as a vast and agitated primeval entity fully roused from slumber. Awake and angry.

Greg pounded ahead, his boots splashing through the mud. Marvin held onto Harris, gripping the man's forearm in support. Harris gasped from the exertion, gazing behind them at times, eyes wide and screaming from within. They passed the old pickup, not thinking twice about trusting it. Marvin's truck was parked out front, and they made for this in a quick sprint. The lanterns hanging from the back porch had all been extinguished, and they hurried forward, their only light the frequent veins of lightning creasing the sky.

At one point Marvin glanced at the roof of the cabin, spotting a dark shape perched near the edge. When he blinked it was gone, but he tried not to think about the pair of red pinpricks which had briefly looked down on him.

Can't be happening.

For all his self-admitted obsession with finding the legendary creature of the Pine Barrens, he now cowered under the realization that he had come much too close to the very heart of his inspiration. He now wished that he'd been a more practical man, leaving mysteries in their proper place.

Greg reached the corner of the house and made for the truck. The other two were only a second behind him, and Marvin finally breathed as he locked the doors and fumbled for his keys. No one spoke until Harris, sitting in the backseat, leaned forward, tightly gripping Greg's shoulder and pointing. An orange glow lighted the back yard. The workshop was on fire.

"Let's get out of here. I don't know exactly what's going on, but I'll be a lot happier when we get back home." Greg's nails dug into the dashboard, and Marvin fired up the engine. The tires screeched in protest as he turned the vehicle around, and they vanished into the enraged storm, plunging down the dirt road and into the dark maw of the forest.

«««——»»»

Marvin recalled the long drive up from the road and wished it were much closer. The vehicle sloshed through the muddy trail, rumbling across dozens of small streams formed by the storm, which showed no sign of easing. He kept his gaze fixed ahead, ignoring the harrowing events which had brought them here, fleeing into the night. Ignoring the passion of his own obsession, and the consequences of breaching the barriers which shrouded the truth. And what was the truth? So far, the evening had been filled with uncertainty, frightening circumstance. But had anything been proven beyond a doubt?

He didn't think so. Except for the rock. If that incredible stone was tested, and shown to be authentic…why, it would shake the very foundations of science. It would be a discovery of monumental importance. And *if* it really was connected to the elusive and unproven Jersey Devil, *and* the creature was intelligent as Harris claimed, then would it permit such a revelation to be revealed to an unsuspecting world?

Marvin glanced in his rearview mirror, his stomach knotted into tight balls of anxiety. He mulled the question over in his head, tossing the facts around, exploring the theories, trying to reach firm ground. Something that made sense. And hard as he tried, he failed miserably.

Greg's face was nearly plastered against the window. He looked uneasy, and Marvin knew he wondered the same thing. Harris remained silent in the backseat, eyes peering fearfully towards either side.

Marvin's attention drifted for only a brief second, and he almost missed seeing the huge tree that had fallen along the road, completely blocking their path.

He slammed on the brakes, and the truck slid forward on the soft mud. Greg shouted, his arm smacking hard against the dashboard. They stopped mere inches from the tree, and Marvin let out a deep sigh, his mouth still open as something heavy struck the side of the vehicle and tipped it over.

«««——»»»

Darkness.

Marvin's eyelids fluttered, but he didn't know if he was asleep, alive, or dead. He failed to realize that his eyes were even open until the sensation entered into his face from blinking several times. His head hurt badly and he was bewildered, feeling dizzy and nauseous. He made out the interior of his truck after several painful moments, but everything seemed distorted.

Then he remembered the accident...

Their flight into the forest, the downed tree and the truck stopping abruptly to avoid the collision. But they hadn't collided, or had they? He couldn't recall, his mind was reeling, his body probably going into shock.

Marvin hurt. His entire body was bruised, and he couldn't move. He was facing backwards, he realized. The accident had pushed the truck to the side, turning it upside down. But they had avoided the tree...

The backseat was empty. Harris, where was Harris? He tried to call out, but his throat was silent, barren. No words would come. Maybe Harris had crawled out. Marvin moved his arms and legs, thankful that he still felt them. He nearly passed out several times, and then he remembered Greg.

Shifting his neck, he looked for his friend.

There was Greg, laying halfway through the broken passenger window. His legs were partly inside. He groaned, and was kicking lightly with one foot. Marvin felt a huge sense of relief that Greg was still alive. And Harris? He'd probably crawled out...

Or maybe not, Marvin thought. What if he'd been taken? Harris believed the rock should not have left the cave.

Marvin felt chills crawl along his back. Terror held him close, and the pain was bad. He closed his eyes, feeling consciousness slipping away. His thoughts were black. Had the Jersey Devil acted to protect its secret, bringing retribution upon the older man? Making sure that his story would never be told? There was no way of knowing anything, not until they could escape and find help. If it were true though, maybe he and Greg would be left alone by the creature.

Madness.

Truth?

Both or neither...His head throbbed. Darkness and pain.

Time slipped by, he sensed.

He was unsure if he'd actually passed out or not, but when he opened his eyes again, Greg was gone.

Confused, Marvin tried calling out, the words no more than a whisper.

"Greg..."

There was no response. Marvin struggled, attempting to free himself. Surely Greg would help him out. Where was he? Dark suspicions again crept into his mind. Harris had warned them. Were they now marked as well?

The horror gripped Marvin, took him within its shroud, and squeezed. He fought to free himself, leave the truck and the woods far behind. The pain was unrelenting, but he could move his limbs at least. He pushed the door and it gave way.

The rain had lessened, but lightning still streaked across the sky. The woods brooded around him, concealing shadows and secrets. Marvin gouged at the soft turf, crawling away from the vehicle. Mud splattered in his face. He spotted the fallen tree as lightning flashed, and he tried to stand, feeling sharp pain in one ankle.

It was definitely broken.

Stumbling to his knees, he looked around. The other two were gone. *Gone...*

That fact was chilling and powerful. He'd hoped to find Greg laying safely on the ground and uninjured. And if Harris *had* been taken, Marvin hoped that they at least would be left alone.

But hope was a world away from him as he saw something dark sitting on the downed tree...

The lightning briefly illuminated a grotesque figure—a body spawned from nightmares, a sinister, monstrous face. Most of the creature was only dim suggestion, but his mind met the task of filling the remaining void. He reeled back in horror, slumping to the ground.

The lightning mercifully abated.

Marvin heard the soft flapping of wings in the night. Quiet rustling as something moved. A low huffing. And a most peculiar, indescribable odor.

He watched with dread as a pair of red gleaming eyes appeared scant inches before him, the orbs reflecting a hint of sadness, and Marvin lost himself within their ashen depths as the wings slowly opened and drew him gently inside...

THE BUNYIP

Many strange tales came out of the Cape York outback that peculiar spring season, spoken in hushed tones around shrouded campsites and within the smoky drinking pubs frequented by local guides and trappers, their faces grim and thoughtful. An unseen cloud of trepidation hovered above the collective imagination of those whose livelihood took them inside the breast of the vast hinterland, men quick to mirth but staunch when immersed within their respective tasks. Carson Evans had visited the remotest destination in the northern part of the Australian continent for his latest expedition, choosing the Walker Point lodge as ordained place of departure, a small but well-kept launch post from which to access the sprawling billabongs and canopied jungles within a day's reach, the brooding edge of the hinterland a mere stone's throw from the cabin proper.

Accompanying Carson was his nephew Lorne, assistant and travel partner on the senior man's seemingly endless quests for knowledge, escapades which led them to the far corners of the known and unknown world alike, whether it be among the mysterious and spectacular stone monuments of Easter Island, or the steamy fissures of Western Pacific volcanoes, slumbering behemoths hunkering patiently over molten violence—there existed no road too significant an obstacle for his brash undertakings.

His second trip into the Australian bush, Carson wholly intended to discover a rare and exotic species of water fowl, and subsequently credit himself of finding yet another previously unrevealed creature. Employed by the esteemable *Painted Horizon Journal,* a quarterly-published magazine based in southern Maine, he was their 'favorite son,' his leash invisible, his budgetary restraints an unreachable fantasy for the novices in the field, a topic of grudging respect from elder colleagues ferreted within the competitive publications.

A tanned, dour-faced man greeted them at the front deck as they stood with baggage at their feet. Shaking their hands with a strong, callused grip was Roger Herth, the most seasoned tracker the lodge employed. He had a drooping mustache, and quiet azure eyes which never seemed to blink. Although dry of humor, the man was not unfriendly, but instead serious and attentive, possessed with a warm Australian character, concerned for those placed under his care. Clearly he was different than his countrymen in his reserved behavior, and he made for quite an intriguing character in the eyes of the two adventure seekers.

Exchanging curt pleasantries, they entered through the tall screen door, and Carson immediately set to task, politely assaulting the owner of the lodge, one Jared Conner with a barrage of questions, displaying his unquenchable thirst for knowledge concerning the vastnesses of the bordering swampland, imploring the man to extend the scope of their coming venture by probing deeper into the waiting territory than they had previously agreed upon. The man's leathered face was impassive, tilting his head to the side at intervals, pressed by Carson's impetuous mannerisms.

Lorne feigned disinterest, accustomed to his uncle's impulsiveness, and gazed out at the orange cracks of fading sunlight being consumed by the encroaching curtain of nightfall. A ribbon of trimmed grass rolled up before the driftwood-gray front porch of the lodge, and he followed the end until it clashed with an irregular border of high reeds and cattails clustered about the posts of the wooden landing dock, a span of twenty odd yards until it ended abruptly against a murky lagoon, which lay stretched out in patient repose, a portcullis of passage serving as gateway to the immense wilder land beyond.

Great bullfrogs hoisted throaty calls across the placid waters, welcoming the advent of dusk from their floating lily pad panoplies. The droning of a thousand insects rose and fell in discordant melodies, their diminutive forms buzzing and shrieking between lichen-embraced tree trunks, skimming recklessly above the water surface, dancing and spinning in their endless ritual of cycle—feeding, mating and dying, their short-lived progeny rising once again from the muck and loamy soil. Water herons glided ambiguously over the restless marsh, occasionally spotting a prospective meal and angling downwards in a steep descent. Lorne observed the flora and fauna with admiration, knowing that the region was home to some of the most prolific wildlife on the entire planet. Scantily inhabited by people, the peninsula was extreme in its extraordinary makeup, consisting of lush rain forests, meandering rivers, lofty foothills and mountains, and sprawling, treacherous swampland. Immense in proportion and diversity, it was unexplored and dangerous to the unwary and knowledgeable alike. The durable Aborigines made their home along the fringe, surviving in one of the harshest climates to be found anywhere. Depending upon the season, the weather was largely unpredictable, varying in mood and intensity, and the summer monsoons rendered any form of travel virtually impossible during that particular time of year.

Lorne breathed in the wonderfully fragrant air which was drenched in humidity, almost oppressive to his sense of smell. The land lay magnificently before his impressionable vision, and he felt the pulse of vibrancy as a single, powerful entity. His skin tingled, a combination of awe and excitement at the prospect of delving into this enormous, fantastic world.

Turning, he focused again on the conversation, now subdued and coming to a halt. Carson nodded confidently towards him, an indication that all was well, and Lorne knew they would be undertaking the journey to his uncle's satisfaction. A swarthy servant-boy appeared from a joining corridor, bowing briskly and taking their largest trunks in his surprisingly strong arms, vanishing as quickly as he had arrived.

Carson now walked towards Lorne, clapping him on the shoulder with a gesture of affection.

"Out into the billabong tomorrow, nephew. Off at sunrise, we'll be led by Roger Herth, the most competent and experienced man within a hundred miles of this sinkhole. Let's get a bite of food and a drink before an early rest."

Leading the younger man onward, Carson spoke rather merrily of their upcoming venture, pointing out the crude Aboriginal paintings which lined the cedar walls of the lodge. It turned out to be an abbreviated night of light dining and preparation, as the pair made ready for the morning plunge into the vast frontier.

Expectations were high as the two men chattered briefly in serious conversation before retiring that night. They knew it would be a number of days before they could once again claim the comfort and softness of a decent bed, and they slept soundly that evening.

《《《——》》》

The following morning dawned overcast and heavy, threatening an early morning shower, and the three men faced the prospect of a dismal start to their voyage as they paddled along a narrow channel which would eventually lead them to broader waters. The rainfall came swiftly, fat drops splattering upon their hooded cloaks, but Carson remained undaunted by what he called 'a mere passing nuisance.' The adverse weather broke quickly, and the sky remained gloomy, although not quite as dark.

Roger proved to be uncanny in his ability to steer them smoothly along while pointing out various plants and small animals indigenous to the region. Lorne was captivated by his surroundings, shaking his head in wonder at the creeping vines and mossy trunks of the trees, their roots reaching greedily into the murky waters. Carson took notes while the other two paddled gently across the sluggish current, identifying numerous specimens on his own. Impressed by the journalist's knowledge, Roger would nod in agreement, adding remarks to further succor the man's quest for information.

The jungle was home to a dazzling number of exotic plants and flowers. Roger spoke in a low voice, his words clearly tailored to his audience, reverting to his own slang infrequently. "The *waratah,* with its red flowers. See it yonder? And there, that long vine, shaped near like an urn, is the *nepenthes.* One of our carnivorous plants."

Carson consumed the offered details with an unsatiated hunger. The man lived for information, and had devoted his entire life to overturning stones, digging beneath mounds of dirt, prying into damp caverns, all in his pursuit to find answers. Lorne, for the most part, was a silent observer as his uncle scribbled in a black leather journal, at times erasing lines with a low grumble then jotting down lengthy notes, pausing in satisfaction.

The heat was sweltering, and the men were soaked from the unrelenting humidity. Swarms of insects clamored furiously over their heads, chased away by the ointment Roger had given them before embarking, the root of a rare herb, something used by the durable Aborigines.

They coasted along evenly through a broad channel nearly a quarter mile in width, the grassy shoreline lined by great reeds and cattails, their forms swaying dreamily as the breeze awakened, sending out waves of warmth to the sprawling foliage of the wilderness. It was nearing twilight of their second full day in the bush, and Carson's mood was one of slight irritation, so far having viewed no water bird he would consider to be of an extraordinary species.

Carson broke in with his rough voice. "Roger, how far in the swamp have *you* ever ventured?"

For some reason, Lorne felt a bit disturbed by the question, although it seemed rather harmless at the time. His uncle's inquiry was greeted by a solemn stare from the impassive guide, who never wavered in his cautious navigation of the channel, his strokes confident and even-handed.

"I've been to the edge of Trevor's Fen which we should reach before nightfall. After that, a number of smaller tributaries branch off, and the bog grows nasty. Impossible to negotiate the skiff, and home to some of the continent's deadliest snakes and other such pests. You wouldn't want to explore the region anyway."

Lorne gazed at his uncle, noticing the tight set of his jaw.

"Ah, but you are quite wrong there, my friend." He smiled disarmingly. "I would most definitely like to set foot in that area. My nephew and I have traveled through some of the world's toughest jungles and hills. That's the adventure of it all, tromping about where other men falter. What do you think?"

The man was quiet, and he looked upwards as a blanket of celestial light glittered across the cloudless sky. Gliding the boat to the left, he steered for a small bank sheltered by a clump of *paperbarks*. Lorne looked at Roger curiously, waiting to hear his reply.

"As I said, the territory becomes rather treacherous, and my first priority is obviously for the safety of you and your nephew. It's denser in there, one of the darkest spots in the continent."

"But you possess a great degree of knowledge," answered Carson, unwilling to let the matter lay. "Surely you know my thirst for a good hunt? We've come all this way, packed on that blasted liner like a bunch of imprisoned rats." He laughed good-naturedly, but Lorne didn't share his humor. Instead, he remained staring at Roger, who seemed to shift uneasily before Carson's persistent questioning.

"And Roger, I must say, you are one of the finest guides I have been privileged to be led by, and I will do all in my power to ensure you receive additional compensation."

The man hesitated as they neared the edge. "Thank you, the gesture is appreciated, but the wilderness beyond is really quite hazardous.

Maybe we can try moving east tomorrow. I know of a few spots where no one goes."

Lorne watched as Roger turned towards him, as if to comment further, and to his surprise Carson sighed in resignation. "Well, that may not go over favorably to Mr. Conner, who stated that you were the most competent guide in northern Australia, and would gladly show us into the deeper fens. I'm rather moved that you would decline to continue in that direction, fearing for our safety. That *is* your intention, eh?"

Roger, concentrating on maneuvering the vessel, didn't answer as they gained the shore, the boat bumping to a halt. Lorne knew what his uncle's motives were, and he listened in fascination at the game being waged. He peered into the jungle canopy, feeling the power and majesty which lay hidden beneath the slumbering, vine-strangled trees.

"Elusive and challenging—don't you wonder what awaits past the familiar trail? Such dazzling birds and animals your country is filled with. Why, one lifetime of devotion falls exceedingly short of the task, to discover, categorize, and enlighten the world as to the next incredible find. All waiting patiently." Carson pointed with his index finger, and both Lorne and Roger followed the direction. "Inside there…And I intend to go, with your help. Unless there is something else that you are not telling us?"

At that moment, a shadow seemed to pass across Roger's face, one which did little more than tweak his exterior features, suggesting nothing more than an instant of reverie, but Lorne noticed something within his eyes which made him start—it was the look of a man frightened down to his very gills.

"No…nothing, just what I mentioned."

Lorne knew immediately that the man held something back. But what was he keeping from them?

All three of them left the boat while Roger pulled it onto the grass, and Lorne removed some of their belongings. Carson appeared unruffled, further prodding the taciturn guide. "Listen, here is my offer. Take us only one full day past this Trevor's Fen area, that's all I'm asking. I can tell you now, I'm twice as excited as before. Enough so that I'll march off myself into the bracken, on foot upon return, if you refuse to lead us—although I have nothing but the utmost respect for your consideration and skill, so please don't mistake my enthusiasm for ingratitude."

He grinned cheerfully, patting Roger on the shoulder. "My reputation is common knowledge, but without competent guidesmen, it makes my life miserable and incomplete. You deserve the proper credit if something unique is discovered, perhaps even some unknown creature." His eyes glittered with passion.

Roger pursed his lips, and glanced sideways at Lorne, as if waiting for him to speak, but the younger man was silent.

Roger finally shrugged. "All right then. One day—but no further."

Carson smiled broadly, slapping his leg. "And if we find some fantastic breed of water heron, I'll name it after you, my splendid man." Roger merely nodded, going about the task of preparing camp.

The evening was routine, each of the men setting about to prepare camp. Weary from the day's journey, the two travelers spoke little, anticipating the coming rest.

But Lorne's mind was occupied that evening, as he tried to rationalize the guide's strange expression, unwilling to question the man himself. He didn't want to impose on the guide—his uncle had already seen to that...

Still, the man had been extremely reluctant to venture into the region, there could be no doubt, and Lorne found himself shivering at the notion of Roger being afraid of whatever lurked within the deeper vastness of the sprawling mire.

«««—»»»

They awoke the following day, greeted by a light mist which seeped out from the direction of Trevor's Fen. Roger was quiet, saying only that their trek would become increasingly difficult, and the visibility diminished, as a perpetual fog enveloped the encroaching swampland. The trees were massive, their branches a flurry of movement as their craft dragged by, and colorful birds flitted from cover, disturbed by the intrusion, small mammals scurrying away into the sheltering undergrowth on the riverbank. They spotted an occasional water bird, but nothing unique. Carson's spirits were uplifted, and he whistled a whimsical drinking tune. Roger kept to the task at hand, wary for crocodiles and poisonous snakes, although the serpents would slither away as the boat glided near, their scaled forms cutting sharply through the murky waters and into overhanging vines.

Lorne was both enthralled and alarmed by the denseness of the jungle, realizing that men were an unwelcome visitor here. There would never be a place for them in this very bosom of nature, an untamed hinterland which had remained unchanged for thousands of years. The primeval jungle weaved a powerful spell over Lorne, embracing him within its slumbering grip, leaving him with the uncomfortable feeling of being watched and observed—even tolerated. The sensation left him uneasy, and he wondered if the others were similarly affected.

Roger's face was one of granite immunity, and except for the passing moment from the previous day's shadow of fear, he was resolute, lacking any emotion. Carson remained immersed in his note taking, unruffled in the slightest manner. He was a man of singular focus and not easily diverted. His success was highly recognized, and entirely the result of his steadfastness. It was hard to dislike the man, as he always managed to appear relaxed and calm despite being countless scores of miles away from help and civilization. Carson was quite competent, and surrounded himself with those of similar ilk.

The day was uneventful, and they paused several times to observe interesting wildlife. They were going steadily deeper into the jungle, and the waters grew sluggish and shallow.

"We must have special care. Don't want to become stuck within the muck." Roger skillfully angled his paddle, eyebrows furrowed in concentration. "We've reached the fen itself. See? You can notice the lack of one consistent channel. It breaks off into smaller currents. We'll try to stay in this direction, and should be all right. The sun will be going down soon, and a suitable campsite needs to be found."

Continuing onwards, their progress grew increasingly slower and more difficult, but Roger found a passage. Lorne assisted him at times when asked, not wanting to become a hindrance. The sky was blotted out overhead, and the branches now connected from either side of the water course, entangled hopelessly in a choked embrace. Lorne felt like the air was gritty and thin, and he caught himself inhaling deeply more than once.

Another hour went by, and Roger scanned the shoreline for a clearing. Endlessly the jungle reached in all directions, and he pointed ahead as the way was blocked by a huge fallen *eucalyptus* tree.

"Let's try the southern shore, the bushes look somewhat more passable." Lorne looked to his side, and to him, at least, it appeared the same everywhere…The guide pushed them towards the bank, and they stopped against a clump of tree roots, mildly jarring them. Roger leapt to the ground, and the others followed.

"Should we leave the craft here, and move on foot to find a site?" Carson gestured with his arm towards the heart of the jungle.

"Yes, away from the edge, and crocs," replied Roger. "We should keep a respectable distance, although I haven't seen any since we entered the fen. Strange…" He looked uncomfortable.

Lorne considered his words. The dangerous creatures had been common throughout their trek, but the past several hours had revealed none of the deadly beasts. As he wondered further, he also realized that the forest was quieter here, the insects restrained. A few birds called out, but the area seemed lacking in vibrancy, much less so than other parts of the bush.

Grabbing their belongings, they tied the boat fast, and plunged into the wilderness, Roger hacking a path with his machete. They continued for a long span, and the guide glanced about rather nervously, pausing at times, and looking backwards. "If it becomes too difficult, we might have to head back—the fen is incredibly dense."

Carson nodded in understanding, but showed no frustration. Lorne shrugged, knowing that his uncle would sleep inside a lion's den if it would serve his purpose. The man was incredible. Dedication and pride in his work kept him young and motivated. Lorne felt only admiration for his uncle, despite his dogged persistence.

"No one has ever lived here?" Lorne walked behind Roger, suddenly glad that the man was so reliable. The thought of being lost inside that vast country was an unpleasant one. The immensity defied imagination, and he envisioned primitive creatures roaming the jungle with terrible, carnivorous eyes, prowling the lowlands for fresh prey. It was as if they had entered into an ancient and forbidden hinterland, emerging into the primordial forest of the world's youth.

Roger shook his head in response to Lorne's question, remaining quiet.

The group continued on for several hours, halting briefly only once as the afternoon waned. The jungle grew hushed, seemingly attentive to the sounds of their intrusion. Lorne felt the tension, his own anxiety confirmed by a subtle change which he noticed in the guide's behavior, who at times lifted his head as if listening for something, and at other moments stood mute and silent, a statue of living flesh attuned to the call of the vast wilderness. Despite the oddness of the man, nothing untoward materialized, and the trees were endless in their silent and majestic ranks.

They passed a cluster of *tea* trees when Lorne started, hearing Roger let out a low gasp of surprise. Carson called impatiently from the rear, and they bustled ahead, joining the guide's unmoving figure, the man clenching the blade of the machete, his free hand moving awkwardly, the fingers flexing in spiderlike fashion.

Before them lay a lagoon.

It stretched out like a subterranean lake, the sky invisible from the snaking tendrils of mist which steamed upwards from the placid waters. The sight of the unexpected lagoon was staggering. A feeling of awe blanketed the three travelers, as if they had stumbled unwittingly into a primeval, reverent sanctuary, an area not meant for human eyes. The far shore of the lagoon existed only within their imagination, unseen by their limited span of vision. Enormous trees ringed the low banks, some of the trunks leaning forward to satisfy an unquenchable thirst, their massive and ancient forms strangled by creepers.

But what struck the men the most was the lack of noise—insects were distant, and barely noticeable. Not a single bird chimed its song. No amphibians sounded a throaty call.

The silence was utterly profound.

"What an amazing sight."

Carson was the first to break the trance, moving forward and shaking his head in amazement. "What a wondrous lake—I feel like we've stepped back in time, and are gazing upon a prehistoric landscape."

The water had an oily sheen, and they could only guess at the invisible depths. It certainly had the appearance of being a much larger body of water than the swamps which they had just traveled through. Several logs sliced into the lagoon around the edges, but nothing protruded from the middle.

Carson spread his arms wide in dramatic fashion. "From the look on our man's face, we're not the only ones surprised."

Carson gestured at Roger, who stood motionless. Lorne felt the cold grip of apprehension clutching his chest, making tiny knots in his stomach. He felt insignificant and weak against the latent spell of the lagoon, and the immeasurable jungle surrounding him.

Carson approached the guide. "There has to be countless unidenti-fied species of creatures in such a place—things men have never seen or dreamed of. The magnitude of this fantastic wilderness defies the mind. And you've never been this deep before either, Roger, have you? Don't you wonder what it's like, what dwells here? It is within the very nature of men to seek out the unknown and the strange..."

The guide shifted his head towards them, his eyes glazed and unfo-cused. "Some things are best left beyond the scope of man's knowledge. The pursuit of one's heart can lead to darkness."

"Eh, sounds like superstitious rambling to me. Why do you hesitate, Roger. What is it you *fear?*"

Both men looked at the guide. He paused briefly before answering, considering his response. "Ah, nothing." He waved his hand absently. "Blame it on my instinctive caution of this land. Pitfalls lay every-where, waiting to catch the unwary. I just don't want to make any mis-takes."

Lorne heard something more beneath the confident words—an underlying, persistent trepidation, lurking within Roger's heart, but he was too proud to voice his concern. Superstition? Perhaps it was just that. And Lorne felt the same compulsion, a tendency to back away from the formidable presence of the wild, retreat to areas under man's dominion. This place could *never* be conquered by humans. Impossible...

"Well, this looks like an ideal spot for camp, what do you think?" Carson had already unslung his belongings, and Lorne sat down on an old log, watching for any stray insects.

Roger inclined his neck, pulling out his own pack and unwrapping the fold-out tent. "We'll make a fire between us and the lagoon, to ward against crocs. I don't see any signs of them here, though. We'll put up the pair of tents on that patch of drier ground." Pointing to his left, Roger's eyes never left the lake. His face was clouded, and he looked nervous.

Carson nodded his head vigorously. "Sounds like a smart plan. Lorne, would you gather a few sticks, and see about making us a fire? I'm ravished by hunger, and we all could certainly use a good bite to eat." He stretched, smiling broadly, while his companions went about their separate tasks, both immersed within their own respective thoughts. Shortly, Lorne had gathered enough kindling for the night, and with the help of Roger, succeeded in starting a cheerful blaze. They ate a few strips of smoked beef, drinking water from their pouches.

Carson lit his pipe, sending puffs of smoke drifting lazily in the firelight, and into the canopy overhead. "Quite a day we've had. I feel like one of the explorers from the last century, encroaching upon a wondrous, mysterious land. Men believe the world to be tame beneath their civilized control, locked within a box while holding all the keys. But this..." He gestured with both arms. "Will never be part of the civilized world."

Lorne nodded, unspeaking. Roger kicked at a charred piece of log which had rolled beyond the center of the fire. "Yes, there's too much solitude, and the jungle harbors secrets. Men are the outsiders here."

"Yet you lived on the fringe for most of your life. What keeps you here, knowing the hazards surrounding you?" Lorne spoke quietly, intrigued by the man's reserved nature.

"There is indeed a magic about this place, and a fascination for those who thirst for knowledge." Roger pointed at Carson, who was yawning widely, his eyes fluttering. "I respect the wild, and admire the beauty here, accept the darkness. There is no law, except of survival. It's clear, balanced. The world of man is more complex, and frightening."

"Ah, so you choose the mundane simplicity of the bush." Carson chimed dreamily. "Over the madness of modern society. How romantic, and commendable. We're not so different, my friend. As you can see, my heart is restless, and I'm always searching for places where the wind has never felt the touch of man's corruption, or tasted the acid bitterness of war. Always looking, and hoping..." He drifted off, his words growing quiet.

"You call me romantic?" A questioning look crossed Roger's face, but Carson only closed his eyes.

They sat in silence for a few minutes, each of them unwilling to break the invisible but powerful spell weaved about them from the shadowed jungle. Flames licked upwards, and a fresh piece of wood caught flame and crackled, sending sparks to either side.

Carson suddenly stood, walking towards the larger tent. "Unfortunately, my limbs falter against the labors and passion for such adventure, and they need constant replenishment. Good night."

The other two wished him the same as he vanished into one of the tents. Lorne found himself pondering their short conversation. "What else entices you, Roger? The jungle is so vast, and dark. There is much to fear here."

The guide gently lifted his head. "Respect, but never fear. That path leads to panic and disaster."

Lorne sensed more beneath the man's comments, a subtle unease, surely related to the look of dismay he'd seen within Roger's eyes earlier that day. The man spoke confidently, but a shadow lurked under his cloak of indifference. He was curious as to the source of Roger's consternation, and chided himself for wanting to pursue it further. But Lorne was a seeker of answers, similar in manner to his uncle, and not easily dissuaded.

"You seemed to have some degree of concern before, when my uncle first mentioned journeying to this region."

Roger peered deeply into his eyes, measuring him, although Lorne felt no hint of antagonism. "Ah, your age defies your perception." The guide smirked, the first indication of actual mirth that Lorne had seen on his face since they had undertaken the trek. "You're right, of course. Blame it on the backwoods tales of my youth. This area has always been a spawning ground for legends."

"Superstitions, then? Well, we have plenty of our own in the States. I could tell you enough to fill a bucket." Lorne grinned, realizing that the guide was not so implacable as he appeared. It made him more approachable, seen in such a light. "Tell me more."

Roger breathed deeply, staring into the crackling blaze. "Well, the Aborigines are rich in folklore and interesting stories, as you might know. They believe that everything originated, developed, from one great beginning. It's called the Aboriginal Dreamtime." Roger's voice lowered.

Bemused, Lorne replied. "I do know a little of this, my uncle more."

"Your uncle possesses a great deal of knowledge about a number of things. He's a very persistent fellow." Roger nodded wryly.

"You don't know just how persistent he can be." Lorne chuckled. "Try living with him. It's a constant adventure, regardless of the geography. But I wouldn't have it any other way."

"You both compliment the other," Roger added.

"That could very well be true…" Lorne nodded, then grew more serious. "So, I suppose this land is haunted by spirits or such."

Roger stared into the embers, eyes unfocused, his face obscured. "Jungle shades, mythical beasts, demons. The forest is immense and deadly, inhabited by many real dangers which roam the trees and billabongs. The Aborigines created even more, maybe to put a face upon the twilight, and the unknown. Familiarize the unexplainable in some distorted way. Humans possess that terrible need to *comprehend* everything, rationalize the fantastic. Yes, the darkness. Man has always placed the greatest fear on things which walk the earth when the sun goes down, and the night awakens…"

Lorne felt a chill, suddenly very much aware of their precarious situation, days away from even the remotest help available, and this from the outlying lodges.

Nightfall claimed the hinterland to itself, wrapping invisible arms over the swampland and taking all into its voluminous breast, stirring the seeds of doubt and apprehension from slumber, tweaking them and breathing life where there had been only possibility.

They sat there in silence for long moments, and Lorne listened to the sounds of the jungle. The insects hummed and chirped, but seemed to be subdued in a fashion, and the call of night birds was distant and infrequent. The lagoon lay before them like a gateway into oblivion, and he felt an insatiable appetite to know what waited beyond, but at the same moment he was terrified by the magnitude of the wilderness.

Both men seemed unwilling to continue the conversation, steeped within their own imaginations. When Roger finally moved, tossing enough wood onto the pile to his satisfaction, Lorne felt the weariness in his bones, and wished the guide a restful evening, retiring for the night into the larger tent, where Carson was snoring lightly.

A heaviness lay upon his heart for a long time before he at last succumbed to sleep, the wings of nightmares beating quietly at the fringe of his awareness, arms spread wide in welcome.

《《—》》

The maw of darkness descended patiently upon the small campsite, cracks of night claiming victory as the fire dwindled steadily, an insignificant and forlorn flicker of light in that vast and impregnable wilderness, a solitary glimmer of civilization daring to impose on regions which ignored men as another crawling and pathetic life form, unimportant when compared to the immensely greater reaches of time in which the world had existed, and would continue to exist long after men were less than a memory.

A dreadful silence enveloped the area, encompassing all creatures and insect life which dwelt therein, quieting their murmurs, cowering their movements. The trees were hushed as they slumbered about the water's edge, a ghostly wind snaking between the dense forest canopy, leaves twitching, branches creaking, ferns billowing in disturbed repose. The breeze blew across the fire, stirring ashes and scattering the trailing vapors of smoke. The entire swampland was a singular entity— watching the sleeping intruders, and waiting.

From somewhere in the unseen midst of the lagoon a soft splashing sounded, ending quickly, but enough to fracture the aura of serenity. Moments later small waves lapped onto the shoreline, residue of whatever movement had broken the pristine stillness. A mist hovered above the water, a lethargic cloud of impenetrable vapor, consuming air and liquid like a shrouded dragon, casting its pall over the primeval landscape.

The region was utterly quiet.

Inside the small tents, the men remained sleeping, although Roger tossed in fitful unrest, plagued by ill dreams.

Without warning, a most terrible sound ravaged the area, a harsh bellowing piercing the quiet from the middle of the lagoon—three short booming coughs, the echoes carrying the remnants of this indescribable sound before swiftly dying across the jungle.

Lorne trembled, sticky with a sweat reeking of night terror. He crawled through the flap, his frightened eyes reflecting the orange glow from the dwindling blaze. Standing, he stumbled forward, ears straining to capture a sound which had assaulted his repose—a fantastic and hideous yell from some unknown source. He stared at the lagoon, shivers crawling the length of his spine, latching on with a thousand invisible fingers of ice, pricking, tapping, tormenting him with horrific suggestion.

Roger was already outside, and Lorne stared at his stump-like figure, crouched in the shadows. The man was focused on the waters, peering into the gloom, his breathing the only noise in that vast and impregnable jungle.

Lorne stared at him, and for several long moments he remained in this posture, his ears lying to him, creating mind-noises which did not exist. He ignored the deceitful phantoms, probing the night for any indication of something far more real, and sinister. Nothing materialized, and he paused, victimized by self-doubt.

Lorne moved forward. "What is it, man?"

The guide pivoted, gasping in surprise at the unexpected intrusion into his own watchful reverie.

Quickly regaining his composure, Roger made a curt gesture with his hand, signaling for silence. Bewildered, Lorne quietly approached, skirting the fire and joining the terrified guide. He noticed the pallor of the other man's face, the drained whiteness of his skin, lurid in the half-light of the flickering campfire.

"Anything wrong…"

Lorne never finished his sentence as Roger gripped his shoulder forcefully, holding a finger to his mouth and pointing towards the lagoon with his free hand. Lorne followed the indicated direction, his own heart racing as he realized the guide had the look of someone scared to the depths of his very soul.

Lorne was still groggy after being awakened himself, although he failed to understand what exactly had disturbed him, and he'd left the tent more in curiosity than fear. The expression and subsequent actions of the guide had drastically altered his emotion, however, and he quivered from apprehension and uncertainty, lacking any justifiable reason for such except the visual torment of his companion.

They both gazed out upon the lethargic waters, their combined breathing the solitary noise within the dark and oppressive jungle. Lorne had faced isolation before, on several continents, within extreme environments and under drastic conditions. Hurricanes in the West Indies. Floods in the mud villages of Asia, nearly drowning as angry rivers erupted over eroded banks at the whim of the unforgiving monsoons. Frozen despair on the Tibetan mountains, led by silent tribesmen who listened to the wind and sang to the stars. Jungles were well-known to him also, having accompanied his uncle upon countless escapades stretching the length of the globe.

Despite these experiences, Lorne felt a most unpleasant sensation, one of pure and utter terror, as a feeling of lurking dread heaved itself up from the murky bottom of the lagoon, reached out into the night with tendrils of invisible fear and touched him, probing and identifying him as an unwelcome mortal, someone who dared infringe upon that loneliest of regions, the sacred heart of the wilderness and nature itself.

He was daunted, and retreated a step.

Roger obviously was overwhelmed by the same feeling of trepidation and stood riveted, eyes never leaving the water. Lorne's heart pattered in quickening beats as his apprehension continued to grow. He was ready to shriek his outrage at the madness, but instantly knew it would be a horrible mistake. There was *something* watching and measuring them, an intelligent and malevolent presence, unseen, unknown. Instinctively he realized this most hideous of facts, his outer senses blind and ignorant, his inner ones blazing with conviction.

They remained encased within their stances, a pair of rigid silhouettes against the backdrop of hunched foliage illuminated by the choking fire. Gnarled stumps they might have passed for, if one happened to glance upon their unmoving forms.

"What's out there?" Lorne hissed. He paused uncomfortably. "Can you see *it?*" The words drawled from his lips, harsh and terribly loud. Roger's fingers grappled the air, an absent gesture of nerves gutted raw. Lorne broke his gaze away from the lagoon. Either that or lose his mind. Staring at the guide, he was certain the man knew, or at least suspected the source of their fear. And a far worse thought assaulted him...If someone of Roger's training and persuasion was so undermined by the notion of whatever waited out in the lagoon, then it must be something of an extremely horrendous nature.

Wild beast, croc? Swamp native? All these things reared up in Lorne's imagination, the entirety shattered by his already-drawn conclusion. It was something totally beyond his understanding, which could so penetrate into his own psyche, unraveling logic and courage in one singular attack.

Even as these dire thoughts terrorized Lorne's mind, something profoundly unexpected occurred. A trio of powerful coughs ripped across the surface of the water, splintering the unearthly silence, nearly toppling him in astonishment and dismay.

Roger bolted, a strangled scream ripping from his throat with a deafening and ghastly shout of forsaken horror. "*It's here...*Go!"

Lorne, shocked by the man's reaction, faltered in the twilight, flailing with his arms as if physically attacked. The guide crashed through the brush and forbidding trees, hurtling into the darkness and disappearing. At the same moment, another noise answered the bizarre event, crushing Lorne where he stood.

A tremendous bellowing erupted from the black heart of the lagoon, as if some untamed and fiercesome creature had been loosened from a bitter captivity, now free to stalk the wilderness once more. Lorne heard the sound of splashing from the hidden recesses of the water, and a monstrous roar which could only have belonged to a great beast at hunt, following the trail of fresh prey.

Frightened beyond description, stricken by fear, he was unable to act.

Carson now emerged into the light, his face grave and fully alert. "What the devil is going on?"

Lorne stumbled to his knees, his only thought of escaping from whatever had awakened within the lagoon. Scattered phrases blurted from his mouth, and he shook his head in terror, pointing behind him. The jungle had grown quiet again, and no other sound reached their hearing.

The silence was ominous.

Carson knew immediately that something was dreadfully wrong upon seeing his nephew's fear and bewilderment. He brandished his rifle, scanning the surrounding jungle for the source of danger. "Roger," he called out in a low voice. He tried several more times but there was no response.

Confused, Carson remained alert, but soon attended to his nephew. After a few moments of trying to calm him, he sat Lorne on the ground, pouring harsh liquor down his throat. Lorne kept his back to the forest, and it took several minutes before he regained his senses enough to speak, despite the comforting words of his uncle.

"We have to leave—something horrible is out in the lagoon, and it scared Roger off!" Lorne spoke quickly to his uncle, who kicked additional kindling onto the fire, which raged with new life.

"Easy there, let's not panic." Carson realized that an extraordinary event had occurred, but he wasn't about to give way to fear and madness. "He left through there—back the way we arrived?" He gestured into the jungle.

Lorne nodded furiously, gazing towards the water's edge, expecting at any moment to see the shadow of his nightmares materialize and step into the light.

Carson shook his head in bewilderment. "Damn, it makes no sense—why, none at all! The man is one of the finest guides I've ever seen, his reputation immaculate. And he ran away just like that? Outrageous! I never heard of such nonsense. Now, what exactly did you hear?"

Lorne described the sound, and his feeling of dread, relating the events leading up to Roger's flight. The horror held him tightly, and only the strong and reliable presence of his uncle kept him from losing his own wits and go mad, or worse yet, run off into oblivion himself.

"Dawn is still a good two hours or more away, and we can't risk going after him into the brush. We'll wait and see if he returns." Carson knelt down next to his nephew, holding the rifle in the crook of his arm, never taking his eyes off the stale waters.

"But something is out in that lagoon. We have to go." Lorne fingered a small pistol, still frightened, but his emotions were more controlled now, his uncle restraining his terror and channeling it into manageable limits.

"You heard something, I've no doubt of that. Perhaps a large crocodile, or even several of them. We'll be all right with the fire, and our weapons. You needn't worry. But that still doesn't explain Roger's actions, though. Outrageous…"

"It was like nothing I've ever heard before," Lorne said, his voice dreamy. "A roaring, but totally unknown. I felt strange ever since we set foot here—and Roger as well. I could see it in his eyes."

To his surprise, Carson agreed. "I know. A peculiar look in his face, but I made little of it. Superstition. Could be I've made a horrendous mistake by prodding the man to take us out here." He sounded genuinely troubled.

"But some creature waited in the lagoon. I felt as if we were being watched. I can't explain it." Lorne shuddered.

"And now?"

The younger man hesitated before answering. The jungle loomed dark and close, but the threat felt further away from him. "I feel terribly worried about Roger—and us. But the forest seems normal again. It's uncanny. What in the devil's name happened here?"

Carson gently shook his head. "I'm as mystified as you, my boy. We'll find our way back to the boat, have no fear. It won't be that difficult. But as for Roger, who can say?"

They sat quietly, the prospect of sleep an impossibility under the strained conditions. The men spoke lightly, trying to rationalize the guide's unpredictable behavior, and where he might have fled. Lorne noticed that the normal night sounds had returned, and the surrounding jungle seemed to have forgotten its recent inactivity. Carson was not unaffected, although he skirted the subject, unwilling to prod the strange circumstances any further than necessary, considering the bizarre situation.

Little else could be done for the remainder of the night. They huddled before the flames, as primitive men hiding from the unknown creatures of darkness. Carson tried to make sense of Roger's unexplainable actions, thinking he might have sorely misjudged him. Lorne replayed the events in his mind, unable to quench the feeling of dread which had seeped forth from the lagoon like a carpet of poison, rendering the unsuspecting onlookers into an almost childlike state of terror. The minutes dragged on agonizingly, and Carson did everything in his power to comfort his nephew.

When dawn finally arrived, gloomy and tense, Lorne felt a sense of relief as the wall of darkness lifted, and even a bit of hope surged inside him once more. The nightmares yet lurked, but were much subdued beneath the prospect of a fresh outlook on their situation.

Carson went about tearing down the tents, helped by Lorne, who remained suspicious and cautious, not wishing to be left alone for a second.

The coming of light brings clearer understanding, shedding not only physical, but also psychological illumination upon many things, and so it was with the two travelers. The fears of the night were distanced, siphoned away into the further reaches of their minds, blanketed by the confidence of the new day and their own sense of reasoning, which argued against the terrors which waited beneath the placid surface of consciousness.

Led by Carson, the two men engaged the formidable jungle again, following the path which Roger had cut for them the previous afternoon. Although the trek itself remained difficult, finding the trail was not. Yet recent, the signs of their passage were clearly evident—boot imprints in the yielding turf, thickets sliced through and trampled. These marks of human presence would not last very long, as the jungle would soon erase them, bury the footprints, and return the region to its natural form within a scant few days or less.

All that morning they found no indication of the guide. Carson had faced a terrible decision earlier—either to plunge headlong into the bush, attempting to chase down Roger, or retrace their route and make for the boat. He chose the latter course, the safety of his nephew foremost in his mind. Carson also hoped that Roger would regain his senses after a time and meet up with them at the landing point, or eventually return to the lagoon. He spoke with Lorne of these matters but his nephew was silent, convinced that the guide would certainly not come back to the camp. In fact, he was plagued by the horrific conclusion that the man might not be found at all, fallen victim to whatever had been disturbed inside the dark waters and subsequently hunted into the forsaken and desolate night. He shuddered at the dismal notion of the guide wandering through the vast jungle, stripped of his reasoning, pursued by something unknown. It was a hideous thought, and one that haunted him during their journey back.

The air was heavy, the humidity a weight upon their weary shoulders, and the jungle seemed without end. Several times Carson paused, looking for something to clarify his direction, and would resume once more. The morning bled into an overcast afternoon, the sky turning black and angry. Sometime during the day the trail had been lost. The grass and brush became too thick, and all signs of their earlier passage had disappeared. They continued onward, Carson reassuring his nephew that the distance was not too great to find the landing. They plunged ahead in silence, eyes focused on the trees in front, minds keyed to the task at hand.

The day grew long. They walked through a small clearing, grateful for the break, and once again entered the jungle. Lorne looked up through the dense canopy, wondering if they would ever find their way back to the craft. He was about to mention something to his uncle, when to his utter shock, a face appeared next to a cluster of high grass—two faces, in fact.

Gasping, his uncle heard the exclamation, and pivoted around to check upon Lorne, shouldering his rifle. Two men stood beneath the branches of a monstrous, vine-strangled tree.

Aborigines…

Four pairs of eyes locked gazes, and it was Carson who quickly broke the uncomfortable silence. "Damn it, you two fellows scared the wits out of us. We've lost our guide, perhaps you can help us?"

The men looked curiously at the travelers, whispering in their own tongue. After a moment of brief hesitation, the taller of the two came forward, speaking in broken English. Carson immediately played the part of courtesy, offering them a drink from his metal flask. "A nip of Scotch, eh? You haven't tasted this before."

The natives appeared friendly, and after a few moments they seemed to relax, conferring with Carson about their plight. Lorne was tired and felt light-headed, resigning himself to letting his uncle handle the situation, which he was well apt to regardless.

Talking in scattered fragments in their own dialect, Carson impressed the two considerably. Lorne watched the conversation with interest, appreciating the extended period of rest. After a span of several minutes, the communication was satisfactory to Carson, who at times snapped his head around, nodding to Lorne, and giving him small pieces of information. But Carson's face soon grew troubled, and he rubbed at the stubble on his chin. He left the Aborigines and joined his nephew.

"What is it? Did you tell them about Roger?" Lorne felt a chill even mentioning the guide's name.

"Yes, that is precisely the problem. They know Roger quite well, actually, and were terribly disturbed to hear about his queer fit. What bothers them even more was the description I gave to them of your experience. They found it extremely disquieting…" Carson glanced over at the two who were chatting furiously across from them, both men looking distraught.

"What did they say?" Lorne sat upright.

There was an uncomfortable pause before his uncle continued. "Hmm, that Roger was chased away by something terrible—one which has scared them to the very bone themselves."

Lorne dreaded hearing what would come next.

"They claim that a creature called the Bunyip has been roaming the waters near our camp. And it went after Roger."

"And what in the world is a Bunyip?"

"Well, a rather horrible beast. Legendary inhabitant of the deep jungle. Lives in the billabongs and rivers. The most dangerous creature to be found anywhere. But it's a folktale. Equivalent to our bogeyman, if you will." Carson shook his head gently, unperturbed by the inclination of the natives.

"But *they* believe in it?"

"Most undoubtedly. A superstitious people to the core. They wish to depart the area before nightfall. They think the creature may still be prowling nearby after dark, and might track us next."

Lorne was stung by the words, despite the lack of effect they played upon his uncle. The cloak of fear wrapped invisible fingers about his throat, slowly squeezing him. "Can we leave this dreadful place? I would hate to spend another evening in this fen, knowing what happened to Roger."

"Come now, it's a child's story, don't let the wild press in on you so." Carson patted his nephew kindly, then straightened. "Anyway, we share the same path, and they will accompany us to find our boat. They also told me the river is only a few minutes away. Let's be off."

Carson spoke to the Aborigines and the four men headed into the brush once more, now led by the two natives. Thunder rumbled ominously overhead, and fat raindrops began to fall. Evening swiftly drew nigh, and Lorne felt a growing uneasiness at the coming twilight. The possibility of spending another night in Trevor's Fen was a daunting one. They continued onward for a while, the jungle canopy soon disappearing in a wall of rising mist, which clung heavily upon the trees and hovered above them, blacking out the higher boughs in folds of gray.

Lorne watched the men curiously, trying to gauge their reaction as the group trudged quietly along. Their grim faces did nothing to reassure him, but only served to feed his own apprehension. The natives looked about worriedly, increasing their pace. Several times Carson spoke briefly to them, nodding his head confidently, and winking back to his nephew. Lorne realized the man was trying to comfort him, but until he left the jungle behind, there would be no respite for himself.

It was apparent that the dreary weather was a hindrance to their progress, and for them to venture anywhere upon the water under such conditions would prove too great a hazard. One of the Aborigines let out a low whistle, and Carson shouted to his nephew that they had finally reached the river. Moving ahead, they paused along the bank. The water was sluggish, the far side obscured in haze.

"I think our craft is further downstream, I remember the fallen tree," said Carson. "But it's getting too dark to travel much longer."

The natives looked upon the channel suspiciously, and Lorne observed them closely. The men gazed silently at the landscape, and he realized they relied on all their senses—much more than just vision. One of them spoke quietly to Carson, and Lorne heard the hesitation in the garbled words. His uncle replied, and the conversation went on for over a minute. He turned towards his nephew.

"All right, they've agreed to help us find the craft. They came on foot, and will leave by a different path, but they will spend the night with us, whether or not we find the boat. Let's hurry, the fog is thickening."

They trekked off, skirting the muddy bank and picking a path along the edge. Everything appeared the same to Lorne, there was no indication they had been here only a day ago, or that anyone else had ever walked the land. It was an immense jungle, primeval and unexplored, frequented only by the staunch Aborigines, and a few trappers and guides, and most of these closer to the fringe. They were deeper inside the wild than he cared to think.

They had gone on only a few minutes when they unexpectedly came upon the boat, pulled onto the shore exactly as they had left it. Carson grinned broadly, complimenting the durable natives in their own dialect. Lorne felt a slight measure of relief, but it was overshadowed by the realization that they were still within Trevor's Fen.

"We'll set the tents up here." His uncle pointed to a depression several dozen yards from the river, a small clearing bordered by a cluster of *paperbarks*. "This will do nicely for the evening."

All four assisted, and shortly camp was set. The fire blazed cheerily before them, and food was shared by all. The natives still appeared dour and reserved, but otherwise were of a good nature, friendly to the neighboring lodges and the men associated with them, trading their handcrafted wares in exchange for 'civilized' offerings. Carson took several items from his backpack, including a small flask of Scotch, a double-edged hunting knife, and a pouch of smoking tobacco, giving these things to the Aborigines for their helpfulness. The men seemed genuinely pleased, somewhat forgetting their uneasiness and relaxing as they sat around the fire.

Lorne yawned, exhausted from the hike through the jungle, and he wished for a warm bed beneath sheltered walls. After this trip, he fully intended on convincing his uncle to hold off on further expeditions for the rest of the year. The current venture had far surpassed his thirst for excitement, in an altogether unpleasant manner...

The natives huddled close to the fire, a gesture not so much to capture the heat, as the jungle air was warm, but more to keep away the superstitious notions they had spoken of earlier. They were a people in touch with the land and its manifestations, whether real or imagined. Lorne watched them through weary eyes, switching his gaze to his uncle, who seemed to have hidden reservoirs of stamina and knowledge. The man was certainly remarkable, and Lorne held him in the utmost degree of respect. Carson could stare down a dragon in its own lair, he mused.

Lorne also considered the purpose of their journey, wondering if his uncle was disappointed, failing to discover any wildlife of peculiar and unknown species. To some extent he might be, but the bizarre events of the past night had disrupted everything, and Roger was still missing. A search party would be sent off immediately upon their return—of this he was certain. Carson's priority was to get his nephew to safety, and there would be no sidetracking in their course of action.

These thoughts swam in Lorne's head, and his eyelids fluttered. It was all the opportunity his tired body needed, and he quickly succumbed to the seductive arms of sleep.

«««—»»»

Silence.

Lorne opened his eyes, and the lack of noise sent a cold shiver down his cramped back. The jungle was hushed, the only sound the hissing of the dying fire and the muffled breathing of the others. He spotted the two natives laying on the ground, light blankets thrown over their bodies to keep away insects. There was no sign of his uncle, although he most likely had retired into the tent. Lorne himself was covered with a blanket, as Carson must have placed it there, not wishing to awaken him.

Lorne was surprised as a sudden flicker of light approached from the direction of the river.

He held his breath, heart pounding madly as a figure slowly came towards him from the trees.

Was it Roger?

His mind reeled, expecting to see the grim face of the guide, returning from the depths of the great jungle, eyes wide and terrible. Seconds passed by, excruciatingly slow, and the shadow grew larger.

The figure now stood before the dwindling blaze, staring down at him.

It took Lorne only a moment to realize that it was Carson himself, holding a flaming brand in one hand, the other clenched into a fist. He exhaled deeply, relieved by his uncle's sudden appearance.

"What in the devil's name are you doing up so late? And where were you?" Lorne raised himself, shaking off the blanket.

"*Something* is out there…"

The words were low, the voice tormented. The usual confidence was gone, replaced by self-doubt and terror, and Lorne gasped at the implications. The flames illuminated Carson's face, revealing a starkly pale complexion, as if the color had drained entirely from him. The hand holding the torch trembled, and his eyes were haunted.

At the same time, the Aborigines stirred, coming fully alert instantly, their own orbs glazed over with dread. It was a terrible moment, and Lorne felt the same horror as he had the previous night, just before Roger had fled in terror…

"Wh-what's wrong?" Lorne's throat was dry, and a cold sweat formed on his neck and back.

Carson turned, pointing towards the river, where he had returned from. "I awoke, hearing a noise not from within my dreams. And again, once I left the tent."

The natives were now on their feet, their heads focused in the direction of the water. They gazed into the night, every sense tuned outward—probing, and waiting.

"*What* did you hear?" Lorne hissed.

Carson moved nearer to him. "A loud noise, a succession of cries. Like the coughing of some great beast. It was hideous."

"Did you go to the river?" Lorne watched his uncle in fascination, mesmerized by the fear etched into the man's eyes. A fear he had never seen there before.

"I did, but halted. I was overwhelmed with a sense of terror—absolute, unspeakable terror. Like a terrified child caught in a nightmare."

Lorne and the natives listened to his words, shackled invisibly in abhorrence and amazement.

Carson leaned closer. "*Something* is out there, I tell you."

Lorne made a silent plea, praying that it was all a dream, a dreadful, black dream, and consciousness was swiftly approaching to restore his comfortable world. "No, no…" He whispered. "Don't say it."

"They know—look at their faces." Carson pointed towards the natives in accusation. "Their fear is indescribable. They spoke of the beast. Named it."

There was a horrible pause, and something cold seized Lorne's heart and squeezed.

Carson's eyes looked wild. "It exists!"

Lorne crept forward. "Madness, listen to your own words. Superstition…"

His uncle shook his head furiously. "I'm shamed. Frightened as a child. I will not *succumb* to this fear!" Carson stamped his feet, the noise appallingly loud in the quiet sanctuary of the immense jungle.

They remained standing there, all four of them facing the outer darkness and their own inner horrors.

Lorne's mind raced with explanations as he desperately tried to reason away the lurking and unrelenting terror of the unspeakable. To believe in anything else would be the end of his sanity, and him. The minutes dragged by in agony, the silence profound and complete. Not a single bird called, or insect droned. Exactly as it had been the night before. The essence of the jungle seemed to have been muted, the vitality extinguished. All except for the presence of something else which lay hidden in front of them. Each of them felt the touch of *otherness,* and was immobilized. Lorne waited, praying against the inevitable, and cursing what he knew would follow. His lips were frozen, but his mind screamed in denial.

Then it happened…

Three booming coughs rumbled into the night from the direction of the river. The Aborigines whimpered, making warding-off gestures, and Lorne felt his knees buckle beneath him. He was a defeated man. The impossibility of what faced him was too much for his overwrought mind.

Out of the group, only Carson seemed to still maintain his senses, beleaguered as they were. The cries echoed through the trees, powerful and ghastly. The jungle itself seemed to hunker down, diminished in size and magnitude.

"It's the beast." Carson's voice was an icy whisper.

Lorne looked in shock at the expression on his uncle's face.

"The Bunyip!"

The name pierced through Lorne's chest as grisly as any physical blade.

His uncle turned towards him, and Lorne was devastated by the words which the man uttered, seeping forth from his mouth like a condemnation.

"I *must* see this creature. This will be my greatest discovery. It's what I've lived for!"

Incredibly, he lunged forward, quickly disappearing into the brush.

Lorne stiffened in bewilderment. It was madness! Outrageous, to face what waited at the river. He snapped his head around, looking for guidance. The natives returned his stare with terrified eyes. They were beyond fright, unable to talk or move. There could be no help from them, he knew. Tears of frustration trickled down his cheek, and he felt mired as if he were trapped within quicksand. His dread was tangible, rendering him incapable of speech or action.

The last thing he remembered was another series of coughs, devastating and harsh, followed by a blood-curdling wail of anguish, which could only have come from human lips. Lorne pitched forward, his stomach heaving as he tasted the bile in his throat, his face slamming down upon the moist, yielding ground.

The horror seized his mind, stripping away his consciousness and plummeting him into a black void of oblivion.

«««——»»»

Memories were like figures in a mist, materializing and vanishing. Images played before Lorne's eyes, visions of a muddy watercourse, brooding trees, and a raftered ceiling.

Time was an insubstantial haze, his ability to decipher reality from delusion under tremendous siege. Faces appeared—some familiar, others strange, and he eventually awakened from the abyss, blinking at an orange sphere of brilliance. He didn't know how long he stared in silence, his pupils adjusting to the light of day once more.

Comforting hands rested upon his brow, and a soothing liquid poured gently down his throat. He was incredibly weak. A physician hovered over him, deep brown eyes probing his own. Lorne spoke in hushed tones, confirming his awareness, but saying little else. He needed rest, and food. And Lorne wept, although only partly understanding why he did so.

Days swept by, and Lorne grew stronger with each one. He eventually learned that a week had passed since he'd been rescued from the jungle, returned to the lodge and whisked away to the neighboring village where greater help could be found. Another week he stayed on there, until arrangements could be made for his departure from the southern continent.

He would be returning alone.

Fragments of his trip passed through his mind, little pieces of sights and voices. His uncle was gone. The Aborigines had brought him to safety, leaving him in capable hands. His memory faded as the details were retold to him, at least the version spoken by the natives. There were no answers to be found, and Lorne felt an overwhelming sense of terror when he tried to recall the events preceding his physical and emotional lapse.

After he left, however, many others attempted to fill in the gaps left incomplete. Guides and locals spoke in hushed tones in the taverns and lodges neighboring Walker Point, whispering with dread and wonder in their voices. For many years, the tale was recited, and even a brave man would shudder, contemplating the unknown fate of the respected guide Roger Herth, and the world-traveled Carson Evans.

Those who lived along the fringe of the great wilderness knew with terrible certainty that the small group which had left from Walker Point that unusual spring season had encountered something which was beyond understanding and imagination, their trip leading them into the very maw of darkness and despair. They could not have left unscathed.

For they had been marked by the Bunyip.

THE BLEMISHED LAND

Stretching out my arms, I gazed upon the brooding forest sitting before my shaded eyes, being curious and a bit excited as well. The *Kresher Wood* was a sprawling and mysterious hinterland of uncharted dimensions, inhabited by wary trappers and elusive animals. My uncle Fredrick stood in respectful contemplation, his broad frame stalwart and confident, waving farewell to the servants who would return for us several days after our excursion.

"A witless man could wander inside here forever," said Fredrick, rubbing his short beard, which was speckled with shots of gray. I could only nod my head in agreement. "Feeling stiff, nephew? Your mind may have been put to task, but I see you are growing soft." He grinned sharply, chiding me once more concerning my studies at the university.

"I'll be fine, look to yourself," I followed, playing the game with him, knowing that he admired the literary schooling which I had only recently left behind for a brief recess.

"Books for the mind, but exercise for the heart." He clapped me on the shoulder with a tremendous slap of his hand, enjoying the wince of pain that flashed across my face.

A retired officer from the military, Fredrick was impeccable in routine and protocol, suffering no lapses within the halls of his sizable estate, or elsewhere for that matter. After riding ceaselessly for the better part of the day, we had arrived at the forest by late afternoon, accompanied by three of his stoic servants, now entrusted with returning back to the manor with our steeds and waiting for us later that week.

Such ventures were not uncommon growing up with my uncle, but usually they were limited to the immediate area surrounding his lands.

Vividly I recalled the raucous fox hunts, or autumn afternoons spent in pursuit of trophy stag, many times arriving late to the house in garrulous commotion, with our hounds barking ferociously and my uncle bellowing his great horn to announce our success.

He was the only remaining family I had left, along with one or two distant cousins. He raised me as his own, most especially after losing his only son in a tragic accident, the poor lad a drowning victim when he was quite young. My own parents were taken away at an early age when an aged bridge collapsed beneath the weight of their carriage, so I was no stranger to misfortune myself.

An old wound awakened in my chest and I gritted my teeth in bitterness, knowing the futility of such grained thoughts.

"Let's be off," my uncle said, stomping ahead and pulling the cords tighter on his baggage sack. I followed his bearish frame, watching the late afternoon sun splashing the eaves of the approaching trees in a wash of lemon, a cool wind floating the aroma of lilac and honeysuckle around us in a tease of fresh vitality.

We halted before the vast woods, my uncle checking his compass, and I felt subdued by the primeval oppressiveness lurking before us.

For a brief instance, I was overwhelmed by the immensity of that undefiled forest land—thinking of the hidden dales and invisible woodland creatures that lay within the murkiness. Insignificant I felt, a meaningless speck of existence when compared to the voluminous life that slumbered through the centuries, appearing much the same as it did in an earlier age, reserved in power and majesty, but undeniable in its breath and scope of vivacity.

Hesitating for a moment, the feeling quickly dispersed but left an imprint on me, the memory keen to my recollection. I would not soon forget that disturbing sensation, and it hovered above my footsteps like an unwelcome relative, shackled quietly to my consciousness.

Trudging behind my uncle's sturdy figure, I couldn't shake the notion that we were being swallowed up by the dark gorge of the forest and would never see the familiar comforts of our home again. I began to wonder if he was correct, that I needed a temporary release from the impassioned scholars at the university. Maybe the trek could rejuvenate my scattered musings, but I dare not give voice to these outlandish misgivings, lest my uncle rail me like a daydreaming stable boy.

The turf was yielding beneath out leather boots, soft and moist, at times clumping together until kicked away. Flourishing moss trailed downwards from the trunks of the aged trees, great beards sweeping the tops of tangled roots which battled each other for the better position. Numerous toadstools sat in hushed clusters at the feet of sheltering logs, some tiny as thimbles, others the size of a tea saucer.

I welcomed the activity, although the sweat dampened my shirt most distastefully leaving me feeling unclean and longing for a cool, drawn bath.

We pressed onward into nightfall, pausing only when my uncle checked his compass, satisfied with our bearings. I knew he had been within the shadowed boughs of *Kresher Wood* in previous years, but he stayed on the outer fringe and never penetrated more than a few miles where the going was not too difficult.

A clearing opened before our weary legs, the night sky casting a delicate web above us, shimmering with the glare of a billion gleaming pinpricks and a crescent moon watching our emergence from the twilight wood. Nocturnal creatures rustled in the undergrowth, foraging about in their relentless search for food.

"What a most brilliant evening, nephew," said my uncle, setting down his pack and spreading his sapling-arms wide. "Sleeping under the glorious heavens and breathing in the summer winds. The quintessence of nature surrounds us—but here we are merely trivial visitors."

His words brought back the strange discomfort I'd felt when we had first entered the forest, his remarks speaking the untold thoughts which had plagued my mind. Fredrick voiced the truth and I was hushed, an onlooker peering nervously into a sanctuary of great and terrible things, where beauty and ugliness were partnered uneasily, polarized from the other, but singularly, each an integral part to the monumental whole. When one is surrounded by the familiar trappings of comfort and home, and other people are in abundance, or at least their presence is felt nearby, forgotten is the world around us, and significantly more the incomprehensible universe, where cosmic formations, which are constantly emerging and evolving, sweep endlessly across the cold expanse of space, as if brushed along by the hands of unimaginable giants, the invisible and ageless caretakers of time itself.

Shaking myself from such philosophical musings, thoughts of a more mundane nature called, and I rummaged about for kindling while my uncle lit a small but cheerful blaze, cracking the dried sticks I brought to him and chopping the larger pieces with his small hand ax. We sat contentedly before the fire, warming our hands and eating an assortment of salted meats and dried fruit, washing it all down with some vintage grape wine.

The two of us talked into the night, the conversation originally weaving around my plans for the resumption of school, and then changing to the daily labors about the estate, in which Fredrick took an excessively active interest in even the most minuscule of details, over-looking the head grounds keeper and interior butlery with hawkish alacrity, fair but heavy-handed. He stood on solid ground, permitting no foolhardiness.

I grew increasingly fatigued as my uncle droned on as he was wont to do with a submissive audience. His tone became subdued as he talked of the woods enveloping us, touching delicately upon the legends and superstitions whispered in the neighboring countryside. Fredrick's demeanor was slightly condescending, but at the same time cautious, as of someone passing a hand over a newly-lighted hearth, testing the warmth. He seemed to possess a deeper concern, but did not wish to reveal his true sentiments. In the darkness and miles away from the pil-lowed comforts of my own bed, it was not the flavor of discourse I would have allowed in that place of solitude.

He must have noticed my inattentiveness after a span, speaking more to himself, as I laid down on the dew-coated grass and closed my eyes, listening to the sounds of the forest. Crickets chirped in the cor-ners of the woodland meadow, night insects grated in the distance, and overhead an unseen owl hooted from its lofty perch.

Such noises lulled me into a light sleep, and I rested fitfully, plagued with disturbing thoughts provoked by our detachment and the tales of my uncle.

«««—»»»

There is no perfect description of that period of uncertainty—the tenure of psychological transition which twitches and cloaks our mind as it hovers between the shallow waters of slumber and the encroaching shore of wakefulness—which can adequately explain the precise instant when one questions their concept of reality and deciphers the falsehood of reverie. That answer lies within a fleeting, intangible moment of time, and only then can we grasp the truth, the sometimes terrible, sometimes ecstatic knowledge that it was but a passing dream or nightmare.

In such a state I found myself staring with wide, frightful eyes, my chest constricting as if squeezed by a vice of iron, at the shadow standing before the dying embers of our fire. My body stiffened, frozen with fear. No words uttered from my lips, my mouth open wide in a mixture of surprise and terror. Was this a specter from the dark woods, come to torment unwelcome trespassers?

The figure failed to move, and I discerned what appeared to be the silhouette of a man, obscured by the gloom, and luridly illuminated by the glowing cinders. In that region of wilderness and isolation, it would have been easy to release my composure, shriek like a frightened child, but I was of stronger ilk, and fought down the panic.

"Uncle—awaken."

Reaching inside my blankets, I gripped the edge of my hunting knife, praying that such response would prove unnecessary—especially if I indeed faced an insubstantial adversary...

My uncle erupted from repose in a blinding fury as his military training came to life. A short ax rested in one hand, and he looked remarkably keen—I even wondered if he had been conscious for longer than myself, perhaps watching the intruder.

"Come in to the light immediately and announce yourself, scoundrel, unless you wish to aggravate us with suspect actions." My uncle stepped forward a pace, clearly displaying any lack of fear to the stranger. I also stood, but failed to match his confidence.

The figure hesitated, then moved closer, revealing a man of average height and build, dressed in a hunter's tunic, with several small bags slung about his waist and shoulders. His face was unshaven, and he appeared to be in his early fifties, although it was difficult to be certain.

"My apologies, I saw the fire and believed it to be a friend. I didn't mean to scare you."

My uncle nodded, but refused to lower his guard. "Indeed. That is a good way to find yourself at the point of a knife in these parts. I can see now that you are a trapper—what is your name?"

"William, and you are correct, I lay traps in these dark woods. But may I ask of yourself? It is rare to see travelers, for there is nothing but dense forest for countless miles northward."

My uncle gave the man our names, but offered nothing else. He obviously did not trust William—if that was his real name—and kept his hand on the hilt of his weapon. I relaxed a bit, determining that the stranger posed no threat. He would be a fool to tackle two armed men, but he also appeared to be distressed in some way.

"This friend of yours—another trapper?" asked my uncle.

"Yes, we work together at times, his name is Nigel. We planned a rendezvous over a day ago, and he failed to show. I fear for his safety."

My uncle rubbed his chin thoughtfully. "What is your concern for him? Robbers? Wild animals?"

The trapper looked uncomfortable, shifting back and forth, staring into the encompassing trees. I could clearly see the man was reluctant to speak openly, but my uncle pressed him further.

"If there is some danger, you would be remiss not to inform us," he spoke, leaning forward and giving William a hard glance. "Out with it, if you want us to be of any help to you or your friend."

"I'm not really sure," replied the trapper, fidgeting. "It's nothing that you mentioned. There are wolves, bears and the like, unquestionably, but these can be easily avoided for anyone who knows the land."

He turned his gaze on me, and I read strong emotions in his eyes that made me inwardly recoil. The man was terrified of something—of this I had no doubt.

"It is the forest."

There was a long and unpleasant pause as we waited to hear him out. The night grew quiet, and I felt as if hidden life stirred beyond the edge of our dwindling fire light—hostile, and watching us with patient, hungry eyes.

"I can sense the disturbance, and saw an odd glowing last night, in that direction." He pointed to the north, and my uncle was silent.

The man continued, his voice growing soft. "Nigel was in that region, and I am leaving soon, to wait for him outside these woods. I will not go further for any amount of gold. I recommend the same for yourself."

The trapper's face was intense, as if daring us to contradict him. I was baffled by his behavior, but Fredrick refused to display any sign of concern.

"We shall keep a look out for Nigel, and inform him of your whereabouts if we chance to meet him. As far as apparitions or otherwise, save the tales for old women and children."

My uncle's tone was condescending—he clearly wanted to let the trapper know that we were not perturbed by his warnings.

William chewed on his lower lip, passing his gaze between us. I was about to question him myself, when he abruptly turned about, and started walking off.

"Very well," he said. " But I follow my instincts."

The trapper faded into the thickets, and I wondered to myself if it had indeed been a spirit, so sudden was his appearance and subsequent departure. A cold dread weighed on my heart, and I looked to my uncle for an explanation. He settled onto the ground, staring at the woods where William had left, while he tossed some twigs onto the blaze.

"Backwoods superstition, a lot of nonsense—nothing more…Have no care, nephew. I require little rest, so I'll stay awake until dawn. Get some sleep while you may, we have a few more days of travel before starting back."

I realized it was senseless to pursue the matter, as my uncle always retained his posture after making a point, and I lay unsleeping for countless minutes with the trapper's face imprinted on my mind.

«‹‹—››»

The following dawn arrived cheerless and damp as gray clouds moved in, and a light drizzle fell upon the boughs above us which succeeded to darken the woods and my spirits as well.

We ate a light breakfast of wafers and dried fruit, washing the meal down with cold water from a nearby spring. At first, my uncle walked through the trees with a lively step, waving the solemn weather away and whistling a hunting tune, but as our progress continued, he fell silent and checked his compass frequently, nodding each time he put the object safely away.

Twice I breached the subject of the strange trapper, but my uncle frowned and expressed concern over my unwarranted hesitation. He admonished me for my youthful attitude, and I knew the futility of such questioning. Keeping my reservations unspoken, I gave up prodding him.

The day was colorless, and the rains fell heavier as the day churned on, our footsteps sinking into the drenched soil and slowing our progress. We paused several times to rest, and I wondered how far my uncle intended for us to travel. The elevation increased and the woods grew thicker, a variety of hardwoods towering above our cloaked heads like ancient monoliths.

It must have been close to evening as a rolling mist lifted from the ground, snaking about our legs and decreasing visibility to scant yards. We had traveled in a northerly direction the day long, and were now deep within the *Kresher Wood*.

Pulling an apple from my pocket, I drew a short knife to cut out a soft section, when I noticed the oddest thing. Although yet dark, the surrounding trees were greatly reduced in size. Instead of limbs stretching skyward, filled with thriving leaves, we walked in the midst of blasted stumps, the branches hanging limply, empty of any greenery. At first I believed this to be an area of fire, but the trunks seemed not to have been charred. They appeared ailing, decayed and sickly.

My uncle said nothing, trudging along and staring at the ground, lost in his own thoughts. I lowered the hood of my cloak for a clearer look, as the fog breathed heavily onto our passing forms. No plant lived here, and now I recalled the lack of animals as well in the past hours.

The ground looked discolored, although I couldn't determine what made it so different. There was an absence of the normal textures, the pigments of a healthy earth. Even the rocks were strange to behold, stale and achromatic. The entire region was void of vitality and tone, as if sick, or blemished.

I was unaware how long we continued walking before my uncle ceased, lifting his head and scanning the area like a wary beast. It was nearly dark and I knew we must soon halt for the night. He then examined his compass and uttered a quiet oath, shaking the thing with one hand.

"What's wrong, uncle?" I asked, moving to join him.

"Blasted compass isn't working. The needle is spinning around in all directions."

I looked over his shoulder, watching the instrument as it shifted back and forth, never stopping. It was indeed useless to us.

"What do you make of this area?" My chest ached, and I had the most unpleasant sensation that the air was growing thinner, as I inhaled deeply.

As if noticing the change in the forest at that very instant, my uncle opened his mouth in surprise. "What…"

He stared around, dropping his own hood. The rain had stopped, but the vaporish mist rose upwards, stranding us in an island of nothingness. "I have never seen the likes of this place." My uncle stepped towards the nearest trunk, stopping short as if unwilling to get too near its wilted form. "I think we should turn about immediately, and backtrack."

"What happened here?" I said.

"Probably a fire—I would rather not go further. Besides, we won't find any fresh twigs or roots."

Nodding, I turned around, and he quickly passed me, looking down to retrace our footsteps. After circling the area for several seconds, the queerest realization fell upon us—our boots left no imprint on the ground. The notion lacked wording, but we both knew the truth. I even stamped hard, attempting to leave a mark.

Nothing.

My uncle was nervous—I saw a twitch beneath his eye. He tried the compass again and I believed he was quite ready to throw it into the fog. "This is the oddest thing," I finally said. "The ground yields under my feet, but remains unscathed. What is the reason?"

"Must be from the blaze," he answered. "Residual bark, or something to that matter…Let's go this way."

Unsatisfied by his explanation, I went after his retreating form, thinking with horror that we might become lost in those abysmal woods. I intended not to chance a separation with my uncle, and kept close on his heels.

It seemed to me that we wandered in the murkiness for hours. My legs felt leaden and my fears grew strong that we were hopelessly lost, but the most terrifying aspect was the continuance of the barren region— it had no end. I was convinced that we only just entered the area, and could not have been far from the normal wood. I couldn't fathom the idea that we turned totally about and went deeper, or worse yet, traveled an unending circle.

I was exhausted, mentally and physically, when my uncle halted, too weary to go further.

"We'll stop for the night," he gasped, "and hope for some light at daybreak to guide us, and leave behind this forsaken place."

I shuddered at his words, and collapsed onto the cold ground.

«««—»»»

"Nephew, wake up."

My uncle's voice was a quiet hiss in my ears, and I stirred from a troubled repose, feeling tired and afraid.

"What is it?" Bleary-eyed, thoughts scattered, I peered anxiously at the ghastly face of my uncle, which was basked in an eerie, greenish light. He looked hideous—his eyes revealing his consternation. Springing up, I looked wildly about, unprepared for the surreal landscape that greeted my disbelieving vision.

The mist swirled in lazy circles around the wasteland of dead stumps, the unnatural glow emanating from just beyond the nearest trees. It appeared between the trunks, illuminating the fog, giving it added dimension and creating a terrifying effect.

"The light," I rasped. "William spoke of the glowing."

We knelt together, trying to discover the source of the anomaly. The whole forest was painted with the tainted hue except for one small area, and I pointed in that direction. "There, it seems to be clear."

My uncle glanced where my arm pointed, but his neck turned slowly, mesmerized by the fantastic glowing. His eyes were glassy, and the muscular arms trembled beneath his cloak. The sight of him in such distress threatened my own fragile hold on sanity. "Uncle, we must leave quickly." I was sharp with him, but he only shook his head at my urgings.

"We have to wait."

I was stunned at his words. "What is this light? What do you know of it?"

Fredrick refused to answer me.

"Uncle, please, tell me what it is you fear?"

The lines on his face grew tight, and I realized that a psychological war raged inside my uncle's mind. Always a proud and earthy man, he was now confronted by the irrational, the impossible, shattering all his preconceptions about science and order. There was no doubt that we found ourselves in an extraordinary circumstance—one that defied logical explanations. I accepted this, and desired to understand the events, but for my uncle it was an entirely different matter.

The words dredged forth from his mouth, every syllable heavy with despair. I felt a change in his mood—his reluctance had suddenly snapped, and he gazed about, unpleasantly awakened from a slumber of ignorance.

"There is a whispered tale," he began, clenching his hands at the air, as if probing an unseen barrier, "that *Kresher Wood* sits against another realm—a different plane, or dimension."

I strained to hear his voice, stricken and low in that abominable locale, accursed and foreign to everything I knew. I couldn't believe his story, and thought he had indeed succumbed to madness.

"At certain times, the stories say, they overlap somehow, and a light is seen—a doorway opens. This wasteland, I fear, is the result of such an occasion, and we have wandered into a terrible no-man's land, hovering on the fringe of two separate worlds."

I crouched down with him, the dread threatening to crush me—time was slipping from our grasp.

"If one dares to pass the veil, he will enter the other region." He gripped my shoulder, squeezing me tightly.

"And become forever lost in that world."

I don't know which frightened me more, the ramblings of my uncle or the possibility that he spoke the truth. If there existed such an incredible region, then I was doubly frantic to depart this blemished land and find my way back.

"But see!" I tugged his arm, trying to pull him upwards. "There is an opening, beside that tree. The glow does not touch upon that area—and we must hurry. The light grows stronger."

The green aura had spread, even above our heads. I was truly appalled, thinking that our chance of escape was closing, but he was steadfast, and hunkered down like a cornered animal.

"It's only a fog, it will disperse. Whatever you do, don't move. If we remain still, there is no way for us to enter the other realm." His voice shook, and I felt an overwhelming pity for the man.

"But uncle, it's surrounding us. We must move—now." Again I attempted to convince him, but he grew enraged.

He threw my arm off, and I was shocked to see him pull out his knife, pointing it at my chest. "You fool! Lay a hand on me again and I will draw blood. I'll not suffer such a fate as what confronts us."

I stumbled backwards, knowing that he was gone.

Reasoning had fled from my uncle's mind—old fears reawakening, suppressed by his obstinate denial over the years to all things defying mundane explanations. A monstrous choice lay before me now—it was clear that he would not willingly come with me. I could not overpower him, and faced the very real possibility of serious injury, which would render me useless to us both, but to leave him there was unthinkable.

The glowing became brighter, the air shimmering with a verdant haze, and the silence of the region was daunting. The skin on my arms prickled—alive with static, and I felt that something was going to happen.

Soon...

Filled with grief, I looked down at my uncle and he returned my stare, giving me a withering glance. "Please," I said. "Come with me now."

"No, you don't understand. It will pass." He shook his head, cowering lower to the ground alongside a desolate and lifeless tree—a fitting companion to my uncle in his present state of mind. He was a lost man, unyielding to his own refined instincts.

I left him.

Scrambling towards the opening, I felt a sudden rush of air over my head but I did not turn back. Nothing could have stopped me—my previous inaction gave life to the vigor of my limbs, and I hurried towards the only sanctuary left in that parched land. The light faded and my hope soared as the blackened stumps disappeared, leaving me in a cooler stretch of ground, much firmer and unyielding.

I looked over my shoulder, wishing with all my heart that my uncle would shatter his reverie and follow my lead. The mist lifted a bit, and surprisingly I could readily discern his figure where I had left him. The light was brilliant, but my uncle seemed vague in comparison, more an outline of a man and less substantial.

Was he being absorbed into the other world?

I shuddered with horror at the implications, transfixed by the sight of him, but if possible, my feeling of dismay grew at what transpired next.

The fog parted in several areas, and *movement* came from within...

No words exist to describe my reaction to the unspeakable beings that emerged from the mist, surrounding my uncle. My blood ran cold, and my skin felt numb.

Huge, shuffling creatures encircled him, eyeless and lacking any aperture, elongated shapes without human arms or legs, possessing long appendages ending in rounded edges. Shadowed suggestion more than reality, I knew not from what element these things were composed of, but they were undoubtedly from another world…Gaseous and partially solid they appeared, fantastic as it sounds, and they seemed to be growing thicker, I realized, as they closed on the forlorn man sitting before their indescribable bodies.

My uncle sat with bowed head, as if in mourning, and I knew it would be better that he didn't see the approach of these hideous and unfathomable beings.

The pounding of my heart was painful, and I was unable to swallow.

It was with pure terror then, that I watched as the creatures moved away from him and *came towards myself,* thus dispelling my notion that I had gone past their reach. As they appeared more substantial, I knew something was dreadfully wrong and I turned to flee, rushing forward in the gloom. The ground seemed to well up in front of me, and I felt like I was sinking slowly into the soil. Looking downwards, my throat constricted as my body fluttered before my eyes, shifting outwards like the ripples on a lake.

Vaporish, the same as the creatures…

I propelled myself with greater haste, sensing a dazzling velocity but I could not feel exertion from limb or muscle. My visual perception changed also, and I could see (or sense) the things that chased me, their formless bodies growing in size to incomprehensible proportions.

Although they were (behind me?), I could see them clearly, as if they also moved in front of me, impossible as this may sound. I realized with a sickening sensation then, that everything I knew about physics and natural law were meaningless in this new realm. The truth dawned on me—horrible, irrefutable.

My uncle was right.

I should never have left him. My foolish actions only succeeded in gaining myself unwanted access to this parallel dimension, and now I was mutating to its properties, but worse yet, I was trapped. Bursting forth with blinding speed, I traveled through space without use of body or physical effort, and the creatures pursued me relentlessly.

And they grow ever nearer.

Time is of no consequence in this world. I may have been here for scant seconds, or countless centuries—I do not know. I am only certain of one thing.

The creatures will eventually reach me.

FORSAKEN

Three horses carefully picked their way up the steepening ridge, avoiding the loose rocks and treacherous roots that strove to thwart further progress. Mossy trees enshrouded the slope, bringing premature shadows to the high country. A chill wind whistled in the bouldered summit overhead, an invisible banshee that darkened the hearts of the three woodsmen who struggled with their mounts to press onward. Foremost rode Kyle, the leader of the trio, and he held up a callused hand signaling a halt.

"Well, Richard, still think this will bring us around the canyon?"

Kyle pulled out his leather water pouch, glancing back at his companion's huge frame, seeming too large for the brown mare he sat astride.

Richard rubbed a thick hand through his bristled red beard, the keen gray eyes scanning the ridge that loomed in the distance. "Didn't expect it to be this rough going around. Let me check my compass again."

Behind him, Matthew leaped off his horse and stretched lean arms above his head. Despite being younger of age and smaller in stature, he was an excellent tracker and could keep up with his two more experienced woodsmen.

"Damn, getting cold," he muttered. "These mountains forgot about fall, it's only September."

"Old man winter comes early to this neck of the woods," replied Kyle. "Haven't been up this far north before, it's all wilderness. No end in sight. Did you notice the lack of trappers the past few days?"

Nodding in answer, Richard put away his compass and absently stroked his beard. "Supposedly a no-man's land. Local Indians avoided these foothills around Whistling Mountain for centuries. This should bring us a clearer picture after we gain the top. Still have two days to make it back to camp in time."

"I hope," replied Kyle. "Our job was to find a shorter path, not get lost in the woods."

"This is a confusing area, though," replied Richard. "The readings haven't been true. Some magnetic interference, perhaps. Strange."

Matthew put a booted foot in one stirrup, hoisting himself back onto his horse. "Well, let's get it over with. The sooner the better. I don't like the look of this place, and that wind gives me the creeps."

"Letting your age show again, boy. Respect the wild, but never fear it. Now, no more breaks until we reach the top."

He reined his mount forward, and they resumed their trek.

The territory was unknown to them, and the logging company that employed the three had sent them out to track a new path for when the expansion grant would take effect, opening up previously isolated areas for lumbering. They continued on, the mounts laboring to make the ascent. It became increasingly obvious that the climb would be too difficult at their present rate, and Kyle made them all dismount, leading them in single file as he tried to find the easiest route. Large outcroppings of sharp stone jutted out, and the footing was unsure.

Tiny landslides rolled down the slope behind them, and each of the men fell several times. Bruised and weary, they eventually gained the ridge and found a renewed burst of energy, wanting only to leave the hill behind. A thick cluster of pine trees grew at the top, and the forest floor was littered with cones, nuts, and thousands of acorns. The ground leveled out and they led the horses through the evergreens as the evening wore on. They wound their way between the trees and Kyle gave a quick shout.

"There's a trail here." He pointed a finger into the bushes ahead where a narrow path opened up.

"Who the devil would make a path up *here*?" said Matthew.

"That's a good question. Definitely not a deer trail," Kyle replied, bending down and examining the beaten ground. "We haven't seen anyone this far up, but there has to be somebody around to maintain it. This might be what we've been looking for."

The group followed the path, which inclined downward. They soon noticed a mist rising from the ground, but none of them brought it up. Considering the altitude and climate, there seemed to be no apparent reason for it. After a while, the pine trees gave way to larger and darker oak and maples. The mist was still with them, and now the path was angling to a steeper descent.

"This is taking us down a hollow," said Richard. "Hmm. My compass isn't working at all now." He tapped it in frustration. Richard swore beneath his breath, and showed the instrument to the others. The arrow was spinning in every direction. Kyle pulled his own out, with the same result. The men shook their heads and pressed on, knowing that nightfall would be arriving shortly, and a suitable campsite was needed. In the deepening shadows the surrounding forest began to close in on them, as the gnarled branches of hoary oak trees grasped into the canopy above like wooden fingers of sinister creatures, clicking together in the ghostly breeze.

The air grew steadily warmer, and the woods were strangely devoid of any noise, whether from animal or insect alike. Each of the men felt a growing trepidation inside, not wanting to announce their feelings, considering themselves singular in each case from the other two. They had continued for over an hour with little conversation, when Kyle noticed great strands of cobwebs strewn about the forest, intricate tapestries of arachnid design. There were hundreds of silk weavings clinging to the branches, and he looked warily for any of the creators, finding none.

Richard would periodically check his compass, discovering the same result each time, and eventually gave up on the instrument. Matthew remained in the rear, and he found himself looking over his shoulder constantly, expecting to see some lurid shade following in their wake. At twenty-five, he was the junior of the group by more than ten years, and although proven in the field, he was unsettled by the solitude of the hollow.

It was twilight, and the men hadn't seen a glimpse of the sun in nearly two full days. First the clouds in the lower valleys and on the slope, and now the pervasive mist which swirled between the trees in lazy circles. Without warning, the path opened in front of Kyle and he stopped short. Matthew reined his horse in sharply to avoid crashing into Richard. A low whistle came from Kyle's lips and he gestured for silence. Dismounting, he cautiously walked forward, leading his horse on. His companions followed suit, and Richard sniffed the air.

"Fire, do you smell it?" His voice sounded harsh in the still forest, and Kyle nodded.

"Yes, from up ahead in this clearing. Quiet now, move slow."

In single file they passed through a clump of bushes which had replaced the tree line. They walked a dozen yards when Kyle gasped in surprise. Waiting until his companions caught up, he stood in mute silence, transfixed by what he saw.

A large cottage lay in the middle of a grass clearing, the likes of which they had never seen. The building was a perfect circle, the bottom section a reddish hue, the upper part a light gray. A thatched roof sat on top of the structure, and the siding consisted of oval plates, almost like reptilian scales. Two windows faced outward in exact alignment with the front door, which was made of wood, with no step leading up to it. A stone chimney jutted out through the roof, curls of smoke drifting up into the blackness.

The appearance of the cottage in the middle of this isolated hollow, countless miles deep in the wilderness, struck a profound chord within the three men. They stood in awe, each feeling the touch of something which could only be described as magical.

Kyle gaped in astonishment, while Richard's face was an emotionless mask. Matthew's eyes grew wide, and he glared at the building in dismay.

"I've never seen anything that looked so out of place in my life." Kyle fingered the rifle that was secured in his mount's saddle. "What do you make of it?"

"I don't," replied Richard. "This is no trapper's cabin, or any style I've come across before."

"Foreign, European maybe. But who in the devil's name would be living out here in the middle of nowhere? Strangest thing I've ever seen." Kyle felt a twinge of warning in his mind, an extra sense from his subconscious, finely tuned from living in the wild most of his years, and it was difficult to simply shrug the feeling away.

The cottage held them within its cloak, a vision of something unknown in a place where there should be only forests and mountains, animals and trees. They were under a subtle spell, but one which they were completely aware of. People were trespassers here, and each of them suspected something had been not quite right since entering the hollow, keeping their opinions unexpressed.

"It's fantastic. Who could possibly live *here*? Have a care. Whomever is in there can't be used to seeing strangers." Kyle turned his head to look at his friends, and Richard nodded, while Matthew remained staring at the building.

"Something is very strange here," said Matthew. "I can't explain why, but I think we should leave the hollow."

Kyle's blue eyes darkened. "What? And turn around now? I think you're a bit superstitious, lad. We can find some shelter here, it's nearly dark. Maybe a bite of meat and some ale as well."

The hollow was deathly quiet, and the mist was solidifying, becoming more substantial, but Kyle was a seasoned hunter, unwilling to give into fears of the night.

"Come on. Tie the horses to those trees at the edge, and we'll go in." He pointed to a pair of trunks which were more tall stumps than anything else. They were gnarled, bent and twisted as if by the hands of a warped mind, waiting for time, rot and decay to put them out of their misery. Matthew took the reins of all three horses and walked to the trees, looking nervously into the forest eaves.

Richard glanced at Kyle, shouldering his rifle.

"No, that would really scare someone. Our intentions are good, so keep the guns with the horses. My hand is never far from my hunting knife, you know."

The two went to the door, and after a moment's pause, Kyle knocked on the wood frame, the noise dull and echoless. There was no sound from within. Waiting briefly, he tried again, without a response. The silence was ominous, and they looked cautiously at each other.

Matthew finished with the horses and rejoined them, still looking back into the woods. Now Richard knocked, the big man pounding solidly.

"Hello, we mean no harm! If you could help us with the path, we would be grateful. We work for the lumber company." Kyle pressed his mouth close to the entrance, while Richard kept his ear flat to the door.

"Hear anything?"

Richard didn't respond, then turned his head. "I thought I did, for a moment there…"

"What was it, someone coming?" Kyle looked curiously at his companion.

"No, it was odd. Almost like breathing, from a large animal, strange as that sounds. Can't be sure." Matthew stared at him in alarm, but Kyle rubbed a finger under his lip in concentration.

"I guess there's only one way to find out." Kyle reached for the doorknob.

"Wait, I don't think we should do this. We don't belong here—it feels like a trap." Matthew moved forward, and the other men were silent.

"What do you think?" Kyle waited for the big man to answer. Richard shrugged his shoulders. "You're the leader here, I follow." Kyle clapped him on the arm. "We've been through a lot, my friend. With you watching my back, I'll fear neither man nor beast."

"Who will watch mine is what worries me..." Matthew searched the woods behind them, all traces of the path gone. The horses nickered lightly, huddled together in a restless group.

Kyle opened the black doorknob and it turned easily in his firm grip. The wooden entrance swung inwards smoothly, and an orange glare illuminated the man's face.

"Hello, anyone here?" He stepped in, Richard close on his heel.

The men had not anticipated what waited inside...

The cottage was magnificently furnished. A blazing fire licked the sides of an enormous stone hearth, an obsidian cauldron resting on the edge. Sitting in the middle of the building was a long wooden table, complete with plates of food and goblets of liquid, enough for a small feast. Several shelves sat against the walls filled with a host of books, and various ornaments that were clearly made from different parts of the world. Garishly-colored tapestries hung from the walls, depicting scenes of exotic lands and beasts. Overhead, vast wooden beams complimented the hardwood flooring. The lower rafters were adorned with oddly shaped decorations, and the ceiling above was obscured in shadows. A single door was visible at the far end, fronted by a railed landing and a flight of steps. There was no one to be seen.

"Amazing."

The other men could only agree with Kyle's description. The building was of a unique design—the furnishings were relics of the old world.

"Whomever lives here certainly has gone to tremendous lengths. How could they have brought such a collection to these mountains?"

Even Richard's normally stoic demeanor was startled by the building.

"It's like a fairy tale."

The other men looked at Matthew. "So out of place. And we've been expected."

The aroma of the meats attracted the ample appetites of the weary group. Steam issued forth from the hot plates, and fruits were scattered about the sumptuous table.

"Hello! Anyone home? We mean no harm." Again, Kyle shouted a greeting, but the cottage appeared deserted.

"Maybe they're in the next room. I'll try that door."

Kyle and Richard walked further inside, walking up the short landing. Matthew had not moved, his eyes still wide at the fantastic display laying before him. He watched fearfully as his companions reached the door.

"It's locked." Kyle knocked, calling out. Richard took a turn, pounding on the door himself, and then shook his head. They returned to the middle of the room and walked over to the table.

"Well, if our host went to all this trouble preparing a meal for us, and wishes to stay hidden, I guess that is their right. I'm starving, and will gladly accept such hospitality." Kyle lowered himself onto a cushioned chair, the arms molded into the talons of an unknown beast. Pausing momentarily, Richard eased his frame down across from his companion.

"Come on, have a seat," snapped Kyle. Matthew had not left the doorway, and stared at the leader. "Do I have to order you? Listen, I'll leave some money here if the owner doesn't show up."

"What if this meal was meant for someone else?" Matthew replied.

"What? Out here, in the middle of nowhere? If by chance another group arrives, then they're most welcome to be compensated from the company—a good bargain if you ask me," Kyle returned. He picked up a morsel of steak, biting off a juicy piece.

Moving over slowly, Matthew stared at the table.

"Coming in here, uninvited, it's not right." He sat down anyway, and Richard took a deep gulp from a pewter goblet that was filled with wine.

"Like no vintage I've ever had before." Richard wiped his mouth, drinking again.

Soon all three of the men were eating ravenously. The food was excellent.

Ripe apples, pears, and berries filled several metal bowls on the table. There was plenty of wine to go around, and enough meat and bread to feed twice their number. They became engrossed in their meal, soon forgetting the strange setting which surrounded them. A good half hour was spent on morselling the delicacies that lay strewn about the table, and even Matthew let his guard down after a while, chuckling with the others. The woodsmen ate to their heart's content, and Kyle pushed his chair back.

Standing up, he lifted his flagon high in the air.

"Men, I propose a toast. To the benefactor of this outstanding meal. If anyone can hear us, we thank you from the bottom of our stomachs. We are in your debt, and owe you dearly." He raised the rim and drank deeply, followed by the others. They all finished their swigs when a faint noise echoed from somewhere nearby, and the men instantly froze, their blood running cold.

Laughter, shrill and mirthless, ending quickly.

Richard kicked out from his chair, and Kyle's hunting knife was in his hand immediately.

"What the devil was *that*?"

They looked around, but the cottage was again silent, the only noise an occasional crackling from the fire, which seemed to have grown stronger since their entrance.

"Are we being played the fool?" Richard fingered the short ax which he always carried. "I don't like games."

"Hello. Show yourself. We want to talk with you." Kyle tried again to entice the owner to come out, but his words had no effect.

"A trap, do you think?" Kyle glanced at the big man.

"Maybe it is…Better check outside." Richard pointed to the entrance, nodding at Matthew. The younger man ran to the door, knife in hand. Several lanterns hung from the walls, and Matthew grabbed one of them. "Watch my back." He opened the door a crack then went outside, while Richard remained at the entrance.

Kyle stared at the man, gauging him for a reaction. His fears came to light as Richard turned around. "They're gone. Matthew is over at the trees now."

"Damn!" Kyle swore, slapping his hand onto the table. "Go out with him and…"

A sudden noise broke off his words as the locked door opened on its own. Both men sprang to attention, expecting an attack from the other room. Richard crept over to where Kyle stood, but nothing revealed itself at the landing.

"Walk with me, slowly." Kyle motioned to his friend and they put their backs to the front door, unaware that it silently closed as if from an invisible hand, leaving Matthew outside.

«« — »»

The horses and rifles had disappeared, and Matthew moved the wick higher inside the lantern, lighting up the tortured forms of the two trees. He whistled, calling out to the horses. The hollow was deathly quiet, the mist damp on his skin.

There was no trace of the animals, and icy fingers of fear scuttled along his skin. Reluctantly he walked closer to the forest, peering into the gloom. As the light fell on the foremost trees, he heard a rustling sound in the branches overhead. Holding the lantern up higher, he saw something move.

As he went closer, a gasp of horror left his lips, for one of the horses *was in the tree...*

It was entangled inside a huge web, and a pair of disembodied yellow eyes stared down at the woodsman from several feet above the imprisoned creature. Matthew backed up in terror, revulsion filling his bloated stomach as the horse struggled to break free. He turned to run but felt something strong grip his arms. Matthew watched in disbelief as the branches from both the tree stumps moved on their own, pinning him where he stood.

A wicked laugh reached his ears and a figure appeared from out of the mist.

"Leaving so soon? I'm afraid that would be quite rude, seeing as your debt hasn't been paid yet."

«« — »»

Richard gained the top of the landing. "I'll go first, keep a watch."

He walked forward with the ax in front. A dim light filtered through the doorway from some unknown source. Richard braced himself, then kicked the door apart savagely. As he blasted the frame, the cottage shook, knocking Kyle to his feet.

He yelled out, seeing his companion thrown off balance, falling forward into the open door. Kyle saw the tip of one booted foot, and then watched in amazement as the door slammed shut behind the man, leaving him alone in the large room.

«««——»»»

Richard was on his hands and knees, the stone floor warm to his touch. He pivoted, gaining his footing, and faced a blank wall. The door had vanished. Running his hands along the smooth surface, he expected to find a spring which would reveal the hidden entrance, but his efforts were futile. Light suddenly filled the room as torches flared to life, numerous racks of them lining the walls. Richard spun around, ax in hand as a low huffing sound reached his ears.

A huge figure stood in the center of the oblong-shaped room. It was a nightmare…

Manlike in appearance, its hunched-over form was a dozen feet high. A misshapen, hairless body was covered in a small loincloth, and a wicked grin issued from a bulbous head, revealing rows of cruel fangs. Ripples of corded muscles ran the length of the monster's limbs, and it wielded a spiked club in one of its taloned hands, splotches of green marking the skin like festering sores.

A low guttural laugh came from the creature's maw, and Richard backed up. There was nowhere to run. He realized that they had entered into a lair of horrors. The ogre moved forward, and a poisonous voice uttered from behind the hideous beast.

"Don't hurt him too much, his services will be needed."

«««——»»»

Alone.

Kyle tried both doors unsuccessfully, and now stood next to the table, rage and frustration on his rough face. He'd been brash and foolish. Disregarded the warnings that were clearly visible. Worse yet, ignored his own intuition. Lost the horses and rifles, and maybe their lives as well…

And now his group was separated.

Matthew outside, Richard trapped somewhere within the recesses of the cottage. Biting his lip in anger, he was unable to help his companions. They were good men, and followed him into the cottage to an unknown fate. He looked around, scanning the walls for a way out, perhaps a secret panel. Nearing one of the bookshelves, he grabbed a text and looked at the covering. The words were in a different language, but seemed vaguely familiar.

Slovakian, maybe even Russian, he thought. Picking up several more, they were all written in the same dialect. Nothing made sense here. But he knew one thing for certain—a trap had been laid, and they'd walked foolishly into the middle of it.

He then noticed a tall ladder leaning against the far wall, and he rushed over to its wooden form. Kyle peered into the rafters high above, wondering if a door was overhead.

Carrying the ladder to one of the beams which supported the cottage, he placed it against the side and started up.

«««—»»»

Matthew's eyes grew wide with fear as the huge spider crept towards him. The creature's forelegs waved in the air, a chittering noise escaping from the beak. His arms burned from the harsh grip that held him. The figure out of the mist came near, and he watched in horror as an old crone approached, dressed in a wraparound shawl, flecks of brown and yellow covering the weaved garb.

The hag spoke, and Matthew trembled in terror.

"I have come to receive payment for my hospitality which you so greedily accepted." Her eyes were twin slits of obsidian.

"Wh-who are you?" Matthew stammered, as the spider was almost on him. "Make it go away."

"My name is Jezi, and no, I will not make it go away. How quickly you forget. A toast was made, and you drank deeply, placing yourself in my debt. And now the time has arrived to fulfill that oath."

The spider lunged forward, biting the woodsman in the neck as he screamed in agony.

"Don't worry, my young friend. You'll wake up soon enough, although you might wish it otherwise."

She laughed mirthlessly as Matthew fell to the ground, the spider dragging him off.

<<<—>>>

The battle was hopeless—Richard knew it from the onset.

Now wounded in a dozen places, he was limping badly, his breathing ragged. The ogre stood a safe distance from him, face leering with grim confidence. Richard had scored several blows that would have killed any man alive, but the brute merely shrugged them off. It was time now to end the fight, and it walked deliberately at the woodsman with the club raised.

Richard made a last desperate attempt to catch the monster off guard, but instead was tricked himself. The ogre made as if to bring the club down, but then with a surprisingly quick move it slapped the man on the side of his head with a mighty swipe of its arm. Richard's ears were ringing from the assault and he flew back against the wall, falling unconscious as the ogre stood over him.

The beast grabbed Richard by the leg and threw him over a mottled shoulder like a cloth doll. It lumbered to the far wall where a hidden doorway opened up, leading to a flight of stairs.

<<<—>>>

Kyle climbed higher, holding the lantern above. The shadows fled, revealing a spacious ceiling much larger than he had expected. All along the wooden beams were small figurines, some of men and others of unknown origin. They were attached by long nails, a bizarre collection of detailed beings.

He gazed at the display with great dread, black suspicions wrestling in his mind that he didn't want to pursue. The ceiling itself seemed to have a leathery texture, an odd pinkish color which seemed familiar, but he couldn't quite place the resemblance.

Craning his neck, he found what he'd been searching for. An opening was tucked away directly beyond the support beam. If he could scramble up the post, it might be possible to gain the entry hole. He put the lantern around his shoulder to keep it from crashing to the floor, and found some handholds in the beam. Grabbing with both arms, he almost fell as a tremor shook the cottage.

The ladder buckled at his feet and his heart raced, not wanting to fall to the floor. He was fairly high up now, and would be severely injured from such a height if he lost his balance. Hesitating, Kyle again started up, and once more another tremor moved the building, and this time he heard something along with the shaking—a soft noise, like an object being sucked into water.

It was brief, and then the cottage fell silent.

Kyle remained poised, waiting for something else to happen, but the episode was finished. Resuming his climb, he was able to make his way to the opening, which was not so much a trapdoor but a hole in the ceiling. He listened for movement, hearing nothing. Directly below it now, he stretched his head into the hole, holding the lantern with one arm.

A hideous stench drifted downwards, stinking of rank meat, or worse…He nearly gagged from the smell, and his imagination turned into dark corridors. He stuck his head fully inside, and the light revealed a separate room reaching even higher.

A noise drifted to his ears now—a low moaning, as if from someone in distress. Kyle pulled himself up, straining his eyes to penetrate the retreating shadows. Two forms appeared overhead, his eyes slowly adjusting. They grew distinct, and what he saw chilled him to the very bone…

Several yards above him were the figures of Matthew and Richard, hanging upside down like human bats. The pair were enmeshed in strands of cobweb, their bodies visible up to the knees. Their lower extremities were joined with the ceiling, which moved in a steady rhythm, like the breathing lung of a living creature.

They both moaned pathetically, in obvious pain.

Kyle was frozen for long moments, shocked and horrified. And slowly he began to understand. They were being kept alive for a purpose…

His stomach churned in outrage, and he felt bile rising in protest at the ghastly scene. His companions hung well above him, and he saw nothing that could lead him to their aid. There was no ladder or rope to be seen, and he choked in desperation at their abominable plight.

Kyle gasped in surprise as a tremendous quake rocked the structure, causing him to drop the lantern and nearly fall himself. Darkness closed in on him, and he held onto the post with trembling arms, trying desperately to maintain his balance. Adding to the confusion and terror, diabolical laughter now filled the rafters. Kyle needed to find an escape—his companions were beyond his help. If he waited, he would only share their grim fate.

He scrambled down blindly, splinters stabbing into his exposed skin. Ignoring the pain, the woodsman felt the ladder at his feet and managed to find a grip on it, starting down. He lowered himself precariously, seeing the glow from the fireplace beneath his legs. When he had reached the crossbeams, another tremor swayed the cottage, stronger than the first two. The vibrations knocked loose the ladder and he flailed at the air, falling the remaining distance onto the floor below. The wicked laughter grew louder, and now a desolate voice echoed through the walls of the structure…

"You've served me well, fool. You're free to go, but your friends will have to pay the price for your bargain. My home is hungry, and two men of strong flesh will be enough. So leave here with their doom on your conscience. Flee quickly, before I change my mind."

Kyle crawled to the front entrance and the fire leaped up, licking the sides of the chimney. The door flew open, a gust of wind blasting the woodsman as he righted himself. He stumbled out of the cottage, heading for the cover of the forest ahead. Insect eyes stared down at him from the boughs above, the bodies of the creatures invisible in the twilight.

The fog had dissipated, and a full, bloated moon illuminated the clearing as Kyle turned back for a final look at the building. The cottage shuddered, shifting from left to right. The woodsman watched in disbelief, unable to break his gaze away from the impossible spectacle.

Two monstrous limbs broke out from the bottom of the structure, elongating into enormous avian claws, and memories of an old fairy tale resurrected in Kyle's mind. A cottage that was not what it seemed— an evil, unforgiving mistress who defied the ages—a black and diabolical witch.

He burst down the path as a tremendous *whoosh* echoed throughout the forsaken hollow, the last vestige of the ancient evil retreating into the sky above.

«««—»»»

The scouting party found Kyle staggering down the slope two days later. Feverish, raving incoherently, the men brought him back to camp, but there was nothing they could do to banish the madness which gripped the once-shrewd woodsman. The company physician treated him, in desperate need of warmth and medicine. No signs of his companions were ever found, and Kyle didn't respond to any of the questions he was asked. His physical injuries were curable, but not the spiritual ones.

Kyle's mind was lost to him. He could speak only a single name, something that was cast aside as the ramblings of a madman.

The name of Baba-Yaga.

PAUL MELNICZEK has been writing since 2000, and has sold over 100 short stories to a variety of venues, including many magazines and anthologies, with several in the mass market. He's the author of a number of books such as *The Watching*, *Bad Candy* (with Al Sarrantonio), *Restless Shades*, *Frightful October*, *Dark Harvest* (with William P. Simmons), *Troubled Visions*, *Ogre's Passing*, *The Rooting of Evil*, *The Summoning*, *The Celebration*, and *The Unseen*.

www.ingramcontent.com/pod-product-compliance
Lightning Source LLC
Chambersburg PA
CBHW020338260626
47156CB00004B/1582